NANCY'S MYSTERIOUS LETTER

BY mistake Nancy Drew receives a letter from England intended for an heiress, also named Nancy Drew. When Nancy undertakes a search for the missing young woman, it becomes obvious that a ruthless, dangerous man is determined to prevent her from finding the heiress or himself. Clues that Nancy unearths lead her to believe that the villainous Edgar Nixon plans to marry the heiress and then steal her inheritance.

During her investigation Nancy discovers that Nixon is engaged in a racket that involves many innocent, trusting persons. The thrilling hunt for Nixon and the heiress takes Nancy in and out of many perilous situations.

How the teen-age detective saves the British heiress from the sly, cunning schemer makes a highly intriguing story of mystery and suspense.

Ned pulled Nancy down to the pavement

Nancy's
Mysterious Letter

BY CAROLYN KEENE

Grosset & Dunlap
An Imprint of Penguin Random House

GROSSET & DUNLAP
Penguin Young Readers Group
An Imprint of Penguin Random House LLC

Penguin supports copyright. Copyright fuels creativity, encourages diverse voices, promotes free speech, and creates a vibrant culture. Thank you for buying an authorized edition of this book and for complying with copyright laws by not reproducing, scanning, or distributing any part of it in any form without permission. You are supporting writers and allowing Penguin to continue to publish books for every reader.

Copyright © 1996, 1968, 1932 by Simon & Schuster, Inc. Cover art copyright © 2015 by Simon & Schuster, Inc. This edition published in 2015 by Grosset & Dunlap, an imprint of Penguin Random House LLC, 345 Hudson Street, New York, New York 10014. NANCY DREW MYSTERY STORIES® is a registered trademark of Simon & Schuster, Inc. GROSSET & DUNLAP is a trademark of Penguin Random House LLC. Printed in the USA.

Cover illustration by Sabrina Gabrielli.
Cover design by Mallory Grigg.

Library of Congress Control Number: 68015295

ISBN 978-0-448-48908-7   10 9 8 7 6 5 4 3 2 1

Contents

NANCY'S MYSTERIOUS
LETTER

CHAPTER I

Stolen Letters

"OH, poor Ira!" Nancy Drew exclaimed and slowed her convertible.

The two girls with her turned to look toward the sidewalk. Trudging along was an elderly mail carrier. He was lugging a heavy bag over one shoulder. His head was down and his eyes were almost closed against the strong November wind that swirled leaves and dirt around him.

"Mr. Nixon!" Nancy called out of her open window. "Let me give you a ride."

The mail carrier looked up and managed a smile. "Hello, Nancy," he said. "Thank you, but I have to stop at every house. Lots of letters today. There's one in the bottom of my bag for you. It was sent air mail from London, England."

"How exciting!" Nancy said. "Well, I'll see you at the house." She added, "I'll have some hot cocoa waiting for you."

Mr. Nixon smiled and Nancy drove on.

"I don't know anyone in London," she said to her friends. "Who could be writing to me?"

The attractive, titian-blond, blue-eyed girl at once became lost in thought.

"Another mystery probably," remarked her dark-haired companion, George Fayne. George was an attractive, slender girl, who kept her hair short and always wore tailored clothes.

Her cousin, seated next to her, was blond and slightly overweight. When Bess Marvin grinned, her deep dimples showed prominently. "Maybe you have an unknown admirer in England, Nancy," she said.

George gave Bess a dark look. "Do you always have to think of the romantic side of things?"

Bess tossed her head. "What's more fun?" she retorted.

The three girls were returning from an overnight visit to Red Gate Farm, where at one time Nancy, with the help of her two friends, had captured a counterfeiting gang. The solving of that mystery had been followed by Nancy's tracking down *The Clue in the Diary.*

The trunk of Nancy's convertible was filled with fruits and vegetables from the farm. When she reached the rear of her home, the Drews' housekeeper, Mrs. Hannah Gruen, opened the door and rushed down the steps.

"Nancy, you're home!" she cried out, and

gave the girl a hug. "Hello, Bess. Hello, George."

As Nancy unlocked the trunk of her car, she said, "We met Ira Nixon down the street. He's bringing another mystery!" She told the house-keeper about the letter from England. "Poor Ira is half-frozen. I promised him some hot cocoa when he gets here."

"I'll go right in and make it," said Mrs. Gruen. "You girls unload the car. My, what a lot of stuff and it smells wonderful!"

Nancy and her friends had just finished putting the farm products into the Drews' cold cellar when the front doorbell rang. Nancy hastened to answer it.

Mr. Nixon stood there. As he set his mailbag down in the vestibule, Nancy thought, "He looks so exhausted, I hope he can finish out the year until his January retirement."

She led the way into the living room. Nancy, although eager to see her mail, resisted the temptation to ask for it. She would wait until he was ready to give it to her.

A few moments later Bess came in carrying a tray with four cups of cocoa. Behind her was George with a big plate of homemade cookies. Hannah Gruen, who had lived with Nancy and her father since the death of the girl's mother when she was three years old, was an excellent cook. She enjoyed baking and often surprised the family with delicious cakes and pies.

Ira Nixon sipped his cocoa slowly. He nibbled on a cookie and slowly color came into his thin face. Hannah Gruen walked in with a pot of cocoa and refilled everyone's cup. As the mail carrier finished the second cup of cocoa, he said he must be on his way.

"I almost forgot to give you your letter," Mr. Nixon said as he stood up, and went directly to the vestibule.

A moment later the girls heard him cry out and rushed to his side.

"What's the matter?" Nancy asked.

"The letters! They're gone!"

"What do you mean?" George asked, peering into the bag. There was nothing in it but magazines.

"All the letters still to be delivered have been stolen!" Ira Nixon exclaimed.

He began to sway and the girls quickly grabbed hold of him. They led him back to the living-room sofa.

"Oh dear! Oh dear!" he moaned. "Only six weeks more to my retirement and now this disgrace!"

Bess tried to soothe him. "But it wasn't your fault."

"It's a rule that a mail carrier must keep his bag with him at all times," the man said.

Suddenly George turned to Nancy. "Your let-

"All the letters have been stolen!" the mailman exclaimed

ter from England! Now you'll never know who
sent it."

"And that's not the worst of it," Ira Nixon
spoke up. "I also had a registered letter for Mr.
Drew. There may have been an important docu-
ment in it."

The girls and Hannah Gruen looked at one
another. Almost instantly, Nancy sprang into ac-
tion.

"The thief can't be far away," she said. "We
must try to catch him!"

The three girls put on their coats and dashed
out the front door. The Drew home stood well
back from the street and was reached by a curv-
ing driveway.

"You girls go left," Nancy suggested. "I'll go to
the right."

They ran to the street and looked in all directions. Bess and George, seeing no one, hurried
to the corner. Then George went left and Bess
right.

In the meantime Nancy had spotted little
Tommy Johnson, who was riding his tricycle on
the sidewalk. She hurried to talk to him.

"Hi, Nancy!" he called out. "I just made a
new record. Want to see how fast I can go?"

"Some other time, Tommy," she answered.
"Tell me, have you been riding past our house?"

"Sure thing."

"Did you see anybody come from there in the past few minutes?" Nancy asked the five-year-old.

"Yep. A man."

"What did he look like?"

Tommy thought for a moment. "Well, he—he was real thin and he was taller than you and he was in an awful hurry."

"What was he wearing?" Nancy prodded.

Tommy giggled. "A yellow coat and hat."

Nancy was puzzled. "You mean a yellow raincoat and rain hat?"

"Nope. It was a winter coat and hat like my daddy wears."

"And it was yellow?" Nancy asked.

Tommy nodded. Then he grinned. "Nancy, while I was racin' I was playin' 'tective like you. I can tell you something else."

Nancy stooped down so that she was on eye level with Tommy. "Tell me everything," she pleaded.

"Will you give me a 'tective's badge if I do?" he asked.

"I sure will," Nancy promised. "Now tell me quickly what else you can about the man in the yellow coat."

"I can't tell you anything else about him, but I know something about his car."

"Oh, he was in a car?"

"He sure was," Tommy replied, and began to laugh. "It was a beat-up old thing. I guess he's pretty poor."

"What color was the car?" Nancy asked.

"Same as his coat." Tommy paused and then said, his eyes twinkling, "You know what? I remember some of his license plate. The first part was TJ just like my name."

Nancy asked excitedly, "Do you remember the number?"

"Not all of it. It was too long. But the first two numbers were 1–2."

"Oh, Tommy, you've been a wonderful help to me," Nancy said, giving the little boy a hug. "One more question. Did you see the man carrying anything in his hand?"

"Yep. He had a lot of letters and he was stuffin' 'em into his pockets."

Nancy realized that the suspect by this time was too far away for her to find. But she was excited by the excellent clues the little boy had given her. She thanked him and returned home.

At the front door she met Bess and George. Her friends reported they had had no luck. Nancy told them what she had learned. As soon as they entered the house, she hurried to the living room. Ira Nixon sat slumped in the corner of the sofa, but when he saw the girls he looked up hopefully.

"Did you find out anything about the letters?" he asked.

"I didn't find the thief," Nancy answered, "but I did pick up an excellent clue. Mr. Nixon, do you know a tall, slender man who wears a yellow overcoat and hat, and has a beat-up car with the license plate TJ12? I don't know the rest of the numbers."

To the surprise of Hannah Gruen and the girls, Ira Nixon uttered a cry of dismay. The blood drained from his face. He put his hands over his cheeks and exclaimed, "No, no! It couldn't be! Oh, what will I do?"

Ira Nixon slumped forward in a faint!

CHAPTER II

Vanished Money

WHEN the mail carrier did not respond to first-aid treatment by Hannah Gruen and the girls, the housekeeper insisted they call a doctor.

"I'll telephone Dr. Amundson up the street," Nancy offered. He was not the Drews' physician, but she was sure that in this emergency he would come.

The line was busy and continued to be so. George became nervously impatient. "Oh, why bother? I can run up there just as fast." She grabbed her coat and went out the door.

While Mrs. Gruen continued to administer first aid to the unconscious mail carrier, she told Nancy and Bess more about him. Ira Nixon was a bachelor and lived in a small house on the other side of River Heights. It had belonged to his mother, who had survived two husbands. When she died, it was learned she had willed the property and a small amount of money to Ira.

But now a half brother, thirty years younger, was demanding fifty per cent of the money. So far, Ira had refused because the inheritance had actually belonged to Ira's father and the mother had kept it all these years for his son.

"Ira told me his half brother Edgar has been very nasty lately and has even threatened to go to court to upset the will."

"Poor Mr. Nixon," Bess said softly.

The housekeeper went on to say that Edgar had become very obnoxious and had almost succeeded in intimidating Ira. She sighed, "Probably Ira won't be able to hold out much longer—he's too old and weak to resist."

"Where does this half brother live?" Nancy asked.

"Ira doesn't know. Edgar never would tell him. And also, he would never tell him what business he was in. Only yesterday when Ira came here with the mail, he told me that Edgar had been to see him the night before and became furious when Ira would not give him any money. He called him all sorts of dreadful names and finally said, "I'll make you suffer for this! I'll ruin you!"

Hannah's last statement gave Nancy an idea. "Do you suppose the person who stole the mail could have been Edgar Nixon?" she asked.

"I'll bet it was," Bess replied. "When you described him to Ira, the poor old man recognized who he was and that's why he fainted. Edgar must be an absolutely despicable person."

The others agreed. Their conversation was cut short by the arrival of George with the doctor. The girls went to the kitchen during the examination that followed, but Hannah Gruen remained with Ira.

Nancy said she should notify the police and the postal inspector about the theft. "And I'd better call Dad, too."

When her friend Police Chief McGinnis came on the wire she gave him the story.

"We'll put out an alarm for the man in the yellow coat," he told her.

Nancy next called the River Heights post office. The postal inspector was not in, but an investigative aide took the message and said he would pass the word along.

Nancy's third call was to her father's office. Mr. Drew was a prominent attorney and his daughter always felt flattered when he asked her opinion or advice on a case where a mystery was involved. In a few minutes Mr. Drew's secretary put the attorney on the line.

"Dad, we've had some real excitement at the house this morning," she said, and proceeded to tell him what had happened. "Ira Nixon hasn't regained consciousness yet. The doctor is here now."

"Well, you are full of news," Mr. Drew said. "Keep me informed on what's happening. Now about this registered letter. I'm afraid it may have contained a large sum of money."

Nancy was horrified. Did the thief know this and was it the reason he had waited for a chance to steal the mail?

"Where was the letter from?" she asked. "Isn't it unusual for people to send money through the mail nowadays?"

"Indeed it is, and a very bad thing to do," the lawyer replied. "I suspect that this registered letter may have come from a client of mine, Mrs. Quigley. I take care of most of her affairs and she sends me money every so often. I've told her repeatedly to mail me only checks, but I have a hunch that she has ignored my advice again."

"Does she always send her letters to the house?" Nancy asked.

"Usually," Mr. Drew answered. "I'll call her at once and find out if— Hold the line a moment, Nancy."

She waited several seconds, then her father came back on the line. "My secretary has just buzzed me to say that Mrs. Quigley is in the outer office. I'll talk to her and call you back."

While waiting, Nancy told Bess and George about the client who insisted upon sending large amounts of money through the mail. It was not long before Mr. Drew called back.

"Hello? Nancy? . . . What I feared is true. Mrs. Quigley feels very bad about the whole thing. We are sure it was her letter that was stolen."

"Oh, Dad, this makes an embarrassing situation for you, doesn't it?" Nancy queried.

"Yes, it does," her father replied. "Having my client's money stolen from my house!" Then he added, "How's Ira Nixon?"

Nancy put down the phone and hurried toward the living room, calling out, "Mrs. Gruen, my father is on the line. He wants to know how Mr. Nixon is."

"He's coming around," the housekeeper answered. "The doctor says he'll have to go to the hospital, though, for a complete checkup."

Nancy ran back to the kitchen and reported this to her father. He sighed in relief. "I'm glad the poor old man is regaining consciousness," he said. "Well, I must talk to Mrs. Quigley now. See you at dinner."

Mrs. Gruen came to tell the girls that they might return to the living room. Dr. Amundson explained that he must get back to his office immediately to see a number of patients who were waiting.

"Mrs. Gruen has kindly offered to get in touch with Mr. Nixon's regular doctor," he said. "She will ask him to make arrangements for an ambulance to come from River Heights Hospital and take Mr. Nixon there. He's recovering nicely, but he shouldn't go home yet."

Ira's physician promised to be at the hospital by the time his patient reached there. The ambulance would arrive at the Drew home in about twenty minutes. Nancy was eager to ask the carrier some questions, but realized he was in no condition to discuss his brother. "Especially one who is so mean to him," she thought.

Ira Nixon himself brought up the subject of the missing letters. "I feel better now. Guess that doctor's shot put new life into me. Sorry I can't tell you where your father's registered letter came from. I didn't notice."

Nancy asked gently, "Did you, by any chance, see the return address on the envelope to me?"

Ira Nixon closed his eyes and his brow furrowed as he tried to remember. Finally he said, "Seems to me your letter was not from one person. It was more like three names."

"A business firm," Nancy suggested.

Again the mail carrier tried hard to remember. Finally he shook his head. "It's not much hope I guess. My head's getting too old to remember things very long. But I seem to recall the first word in the name. It was—"

Nancy and the others waited expectantly. They could see Ira Nixon's lips move as if he was murmuring several names before saying one aloud. Finally a faint smile spread over his face.

"I remember now," he said. "Clear as a bell. The first word was Malmsbury."

"That's a wonderful help," Nancy told him. But she was thinking there probably were a lot of Malmsburys in London or its vicinity. It would take her a long time to find out who the sender of her mysterious letter was.

Just then the ambulance arrived and two interns came into the house with a stretcher.

Ira Nixon brushed the stretcher aside. "Long as I got two good legs, I'm goin' to walk," he insisted.

"I'm sorry, sir," one of the interns said, "but it's a hospital rule."

The letter carrier frowned. "You mean it's a law I've got to ride on that thing? What'll people think?"

The others smiled. The interns helped Ira Nixon onto the stretcher and carried him to the ambulance.

"We'll follow in my car," said Nancy.

She hurried to her car and the three girls hopped in. As soon as Ira Nixon was comfortably settled in the hospital, the girls said good-by and left. Nancy first took George, then Bess to their homes.

"What a morning!" Bess remarked as she waved good-by. "Keep us informed on what happens."

"I will," Nancy promised.

She had been in her own house only long enough to say to Hannah, "What's for lunch?" when once again the front doorbell rang. Nancy went to answer it.

A young man stood there. He introduced himself as Mr. Horace Moore, an investigative aide to the River Heights' postal inspector.

"Are you Nancy Drew?" he asked gruffly.

"Yes, I am."

The young man stared at her hard. Then he said, "Young lady, you've broken the law. You're in trouble with the authorities!"

CHAPTER III

A Baffling Note

MR. MOORE's accusation left Nancy speechless for a few seconds. Finally she asked him how she had broken the law.

The young man looked at her superciliously. She judged that he was not very many years older than she and his attitude annoyed her. But out of respect for his position she said nothing.

"Miss Drew," he began, "you may not be aware of this, but it is against the law to invite mail carriers into your home while they are on duty."

"I see," Nancy replied. "But don't you think this case was an exception? Poor Ira Nixon had been battling the wind for a long time and he was exhausted. Anyway, he didn't bring his mail-bag inside our house. He left it in this vestibule where you are standing."

"That's even worse," the aide told her. "Our carriers know the rule—they must keep their bags with them at all times. But this doesn't excuse you."

"Perhaps not," said Nancy. "I shall take the matter up with my father and he will come to your office."

Moore was not to be dismissed so easily. In a pompous manner he asked, "What does your father have to do with this?"

Nancy looked him straight in the eye. "The law says that when anyone is accused of a crime he may consult his lawyer. My father is a lawyer."

Her caller blinked. "I—I suppose you're right. When the inspector returns, I shall pass the information along to him."

Nancy did not comment on this. She knew that the postal inspector was a very reasonable man. Surely he would understand that the case of Ira Nixon was indeed an exception.

"Are you aware," she asked Moore, "that Ira Nixon is in the hospital?"

"I heard something of the sort but this doesn't excuse him."

"And now if you'll excuse me—" Nancy said, starting to close the door.

With a mumbled reply the officious young man turned and left the house.

Mr. Drew came home early, explaining that he was so curious about what had taken place during the day he wanted to get more details from Nancy at once.

She smiled. "The whole thing gets more mysterious every minute. Listen to this." She told him about the investigative aide from the post office.

When she finished, Mr. Drew burst into laughter. "My congratulations to you on telling him you would turn the case over to your lawyer." Then he sobered. "You are *not* to blame, Nancy, for the stolen letters. I'm sure Postal Inspector Wernick will agree with us."

Nancy asked him how his client Mrs. Quigley had taken the loss of her money. "Was she very upset?"

"She certainly was," the lawyer replied. "My secretary had to bring smelling salts and a cup of black coffee. Finally Mrs. Quigley began to cry and admitted that she should have followed my advice and sent a check."

Father and daughter talked a long time about the whole affair. Their conversation was interrupted by a phone call for Mr. Drew. He came back from answering it to tell Nancy an emergency had arisen. "I must go at once to see a client. He has been in a bad accident. I probably won't be home until late so don't wait up for me, Nancy."

She and Hannah Gruen ate alone. To cheer up Nancy, the housekeeper suggested that they go to a movie at the River Heights Theater.

Nancy smiled. "You've talked me into it. I

guess there's nothing more I can do tonight on the mystery, anyway."

By morning, however, the young detective's thoughts were back on the mystery. At breakfast and on the way to and from church, she reviewed the various angles of the mail theft.

"Dad, do you suppose with Ira Nixon's slight clue about the name Malmsbury, I could get a copy of the letter sent to me?"

Mr. Drew smiled. "I believe so. Tomorrow morning I'll make a phone call to a lawyer friend in London. I'll ask him to look in the telephone directory and see what he can find out for us."

That afternoon Nancy went to call on Ira Nixon in the hospital. He said no tests had been made yet, since it was Sunday, but these would be taken care of the following morning.

"I suppose you are wondering," he said, "whether or not I have thought of any more clues to help you find your missing letter."

He lowered his voice. "Mind you, what I'm about to say I don't believe down deep in my heart, but it will explain why I fainted yesterday at your house."

The mail carrier told about his half brother Edgar. It was a repetition of what Hannah Gruen had already revealed. Ira added, however, that when Nancy had mentioned a man in a yellow coat with a beat-up car and part of his license plate number, he had thought for a moment it wa his brother.

"But I'm sure it wasn't," he said. "Edgar may be an annoyance to me but I'm sure he's not a thief."

Nancy did not comment. Instead, she asked, "What did my little friend Tommy mean by a yellow coat?"

A smile flickered across Ira's face. "Actually it's a camel's-hair coat. His hat is too. A striking outfit and incidentally Edgar is rather handsome."

A nurse stepped into the room to announce that visiting hours were over for the afternoon. Nancy said good-by to the letter carrier and left.

The following morning Mr. Drew telephoned her from his office to report that he had talked to his friend in London. "I have good news for you, Nancy. There is a law firm in the city by the name of Malmsbury and Bates-Jones."

"I'm sure that's the one!" Nancy said excitedly.

"I hope so," her father replied. "In any case, my friend will telephone to them and find out if they sent a letter to you. He'll tell them the circumstances of your not receiving it, and request a duplicate. On the other hand, if this is not the right firm, my friend will try to find the person who did write to you."

"Dad, that's wonderful!" Nancy exclaimed. "I hope we hear something soon."

Her father chuckled. "When you were a little girl, Nancy, you were always eager to have things happen. I used to say to you, 'Hold your horses!' Now I'm saying it again. Don't get your hopes up too high."

Nancy laughed. "Spoken like a lawyer," she teased, and then said good-by.

As soon as luncheon was over, Nancy told Hannah Gruen she was tired of staying in the house and waiting for news. "I'm going to do some investigating," she announced.

"Where are you going?" the housekeeper asked.

"To talk to some of Ira Nixon's neighbors. They may give me a clue that will be helpful in tracking down this Edgar Nixon. Despite Ira's faith in him, I think he's a good suspect."

Mrs. Gruen agreed and kissed Nancy good-by. The young detective drove to the other side of town and found Ira Nixon's little, old-fashioned home. As she parked in front of the house, two women crossed the street and and introduced themselves as Mrs. Malley and Mrs. O'Brien. They wanted to know if Nancy could tell them about the mail carrier's condition.

"He's better," she replied. "In a way it's fortunate that he got into the hospital."

"It sure is," Mrs. O'Brien interrupted her. "The poor old man doesn't eat right."

"Yes," her neighbor Mrs. Malley agreed, and added, "He worries all the time about that no-good brother of his."

Although curious to learn more about Ira's brother, Nancy commented cautiously, "I've heard about Edgar. Tell me, is he really as bad as all that?"

"Well, of course, I don't know what goes on inside the house when he comes there," Mrs. O'Brien went on, "but I know the effect on Ira. He's just all in after one of those visits."

Mrs. Malley leaned forward confidentially. "Edgar was here this morning. Of course he couldn't get in. I guess he didn't know where his brother was. And I for one wouldn't tell him."

"Me either," Mrs. O'Brien declared. "That Edgar is nasty. A lot of papers blew off the seat of his car and he wouldn't take time to pick them up. He littered the street and we had to go around and clean up."

Nancy asked eagerly, "Where are the papers now?"

"We put them in a trash can—good place for them."

"They might be important," said Nancy. "May I see them?"

The two women looked at each other, puzzled, but led the girl to Mrs. Malley's back yard. She opened the trash can and said, "There they are."

Nancy lifted them out one by one. All were

letters and looked as if they had fallen into water. Most of the writing was illegible. One had had the top torn from it, and all but a few words had been obliterated, but the remaining few caught Nancy's attention. This must be part of the letter which had come to her from London! All that remained was:

. . . . .Drew:

. . . .

money has been left. . . . .

"I'd like to take this one along," she said.

"Help yourself," said Mrs. Malley. "They don't belong to me anyway. They're just trash."

"I suggest," said Nancy, "That you call the postal inspector and tell him about these letters."

She rushed home. Her father was there and she showed the sheet to him and Hannah Gruen. Both were amazed but unable to decipher the intriguing message.

"Do you suppose somebody in England has left me some money?" Nancy asked.

"It looks that way," her father replied. "But who could it be?"

After staring at the paper for a while, Nancy began to calm down. "I'm sure there must be some mistake," she said. "I'm certainly not going to get my hopes up of becoming a millionaire!"

Her father and Mrs. Gruen laughed and said this was a sensible attitude to take. "But," the housekeeper added, "I hope a copy of the whole letter will come soon. I can't stand the suspense myself."

On Tuesday morning Nancy told Hannah Gruen that she was going on a shopping trip. "You remember I'm going to spend the weekend at Emerson College? I need a few things and this is a good time to get them."

As she was about to pull out of the driveway, Nancy spotted a battered tan car parked down the street. It suddenly occurred to her that Edgar Nixon or whoever had stolen the letters from the Drew home might be watching her.

At this distance the person inside the car was too indistinct for her to identify, but she decided to get a closer look and started down the block. At once the other car moved ahead. As she drew nearer, the driver suddenly turned around. The next second he shot off at high speed.

"He certainly acts guilty," Nancy thought, and gave her own car greater power.

Abruptly the man turned down a side street, went a few blocks without pausing at intersections, and turned left out of sight. Nancy followed as quickly as she dared.

When she reached the spot where he had made the last turn Nancy could see him in the distance. The road proved to be an undeveloped one and had no side streets. She was able to follow more quickly and soon almost caught up to him. Now she could see the license plate. It was TJ12796.

"That is Edgar Nixon!" she thought. "I mustn't lose him!"

In the next few seconds Nancy neared a wooden bridge. She was almost directly behind the fugitive now.

"This bridge looks pretty rickety," she said to herself. "Do I dare cross it?"

Edgar Nixon took the chance and sped over it. He made the distance without anything happening. Nancy went after him but drove cautiously. Her car was much heavier, she knew.

When Nancy was at the halfway mark, cracking sounds came from the dilapidated bridge!

CHAPTER IV

Doubtful Inheritance

IN a flash Nancy shifted to reverse. The convertible shot backward just in time to keep it from breaking through the bridge.

"Oh!" she said aloud.

Shaken by her experience, Nancy pulled to the side of the road and parked. When her heart stopped pounding, she began to think once more about Edgar Nixon.

"I wonder where he went," she thought.

Nancy turned around and went back to River Heights. She stopped at police headquarters and asked to see Chief McGinnis. The desk sergeant buzzed his superior officer, and after a short conversation to announce Nancy, told her to go into the man's private office.

He smiled at her. "More clues?" he asked.

"Yes, one. I don't know how good it is." She told him about having spotted Edgar Nixon's car. While she was not sure he was the person driving it, Nancy felt it was worthwhile to follow up the lead.

"The road had no signs, but it's the one with the old bridge. He got across but I almost crashed through into the water."

The chief frowned. "Nancy, you must be more careful."

She asked him whether he had any news for her. He shook his head. "Not a single clue to that man's whereabouts," McGinnis said. "But I'll put some men on this new clue right away. Thanks for coming in, Nancy."

Before returning home, she decided to stop at the hospital and visit Ira Nixon. When Nancy arrived at his room, she was surprised to find a strange man in it.

"You looking for the mail carrier?" he asked.

"Yes."

"He's gone home—after the doctor saw him this morning he said Ira could go. Nice old fellow. I hope he gets along all right."

Nancy hoped so too. She looked at her watch. "I'll go to see him at his home after lunch," she told the patient.

By two o'clock she was at Ira Nixon's house, carrying a jar of Mrs. Gruen's homemade stew. When she rang, he called, "Come in." Nancy found him reclining on a couch in his tiny living room. He looked much better than he had on Sunday.

"Hannah Gruen sent you this stew," Nancy said. She smiled. "I can tell you it's delicious."

"That housekeeper of yours is a fine, kind woman," Ira Nixon said. "And she's one of a few people a man likes to confide in."

Nancy did not want to upset the mail carrier so she refrained from mentioning Edgar, but Ira brought up the subject himself.

"Would you like to see a picture of Edgar?"

"Oh yes," Nancy replied.

He brought it from a desk drawer and Nancy gazed at the photograph. As Ira had said, Edgar was handsome, but his eyes were as cold as steel and she instantly felt that he was not a person who could be trusted. She refrained from saying anything, except that he was an attractive-looking man.

Ira Nixon smiled. "The girls always liked him and he liked them, but he never got married."

"May I borrow this photograph?" Nancy asked.

The mail carrier misunderstood her request. He remarked with a grin, "So you like him too—same as the rest of the ladies."

Nancy did not comment. He must not know right now she wanted the picture for identification. She rose, and said she must go.

"I'll put this stew in your refrigerator," Nancy said.

"Thank you. I'll have some for my dinner. And please thank Mrs. Gruen."

Nancy slipped the photograph into her purse, then carried the jar of stew to the kitchen. Driving home, she wondered just how she might use Edgar's photograph to get more information about him. Nancy decided first to find Tommy and went to his house.

Without telling her suspicions, she held up the photograph for him to look at. Instantly he said, "He's the man in the yellow coat!"

Nancy was thrilled—this seemed to identify Edgar Nixon positively as the thief who had stolen his half brother's mail. But before reporting this to the postal inspector, Nancy decided to investigate the gas stations in River Heights and on the outskirts for further proof. She drove from one to another, but none of the attendants remembered ever having seen the man in the photograph.

"Guess he buys his gas somewhere else," most of them remarked.

Nancy was becoming discouraged. She was about to give up when she recalled having once stopped at a small place on the outskirts of River Heights. The station was on the road leading to Emerson, where Ned's college was located. She turned the car in that direction and a few minutes later pulled up to the pump. A pleasant young man came to help her.

"Five gallons, please," Nancy said. When the attendant finished putting it in, she paid him, then pulled out the photograph of Edgar Nixon.

"Has this man ever stopped here for gas?" she asked.

The attendant studied the picture a few moments. "Yes, he's been in several times. For a moment I didn't recognize him. When he comes here, he's always wearing a hat and overcoat."

"Are they camel's hair?" Nancy asked quickly.

"That's the man."

Nancy inquired if the attendant knew his name and where he lived.

"No. He's not the talkative type. Somehow I got the idea, though, that he lives in some distant town but comes to River Heights quite often. He never says why."

"How recently has he been here?"

The man's answer startled Nancy. "Come to think of it, he stopped yesterday. I suppose you're trying to find him. Maybe this will help you. He made a phone call from that booth over there and as I went by I heard him say 'Miss Drew.'"

"Is that all you heard?" Nancy asked, astounded.

"That's all." The attendant turned away to serve an arriving customer.

Nancy drove off, wondering whether Edgar Nixon could have been talking about her.

As Nancy let herself into the Drew house about twenty minutes later, she was just in time to answer the telephone. Her father was calling.

"Nancy, I'd like you to come down here immediately. I have something amazing to show you."

"I'll be there right away."

She dashed back outside and turned her convertible in the direction of her father's office. After saying hello to his secretary, Miss Hanson, Nancy went directly into Mr. Drew's private office.

He handed her a letter, saying, "What do you think of this new mystery?"

Nancy sat down in a big chair and started to read. Her eyes grew larger and larger. The letter was from London on the stationery of Malmsbury and Bates-Jones. It read:

My dear Miss Drew:

This is to inform you it is possible an inheritance has been left to you. We are the legal representatives of the Estate of Jonathan Smith, late of Little Coddington, Midhampton, Berks., who died intestate on May 2, last. Mr. Smith had as only kin a sister, from whom he was estranged, Mrs. Genevieve Smith Drew. We find she predeceased Mr. Smith by five years, leaving a daughter who is Mr. Smith's sole heir by law.

We have learned that the daughter, Miss Nancy Smith Drew, is in the United States, where our agents have been trying to trace her. You are the only Miss Nancy Drew so far discovered by them, and we beg of you to communicate with us.

If you happen to be the Miss Drew for whom we are searching, will you be so good as to submit proofs of your identity, whereupon we shall be happy to make arrangements for your return to England to claim the inheritance.

Sincerely,
A. E. Lionel Bates-Jones

When Nancy finished reading the letter, she looked at her father who had been watching her closely. He smiled. "You were almost an heiress," the lawyer said with a chuckle.

Nancy sighed. "How I wish I was the right Nancy Drew!"

Her father's eyes twinkled. "Then you wouldn't have the fun of a mystery to solve," he said.

"You're right," she agreed. "May I use one of your phones and start trying to find Nancy Smith Drew?"

"Go ahead. In the meantime I'll make an overseas call to this law firm and tell them the facts."

Nancy waited while he gave the number, but the lawyer was told that the Atlantic lines would be tied up for several hours. He turned to Nancy. "Maybe you'll have this case solved before I can put through the phone call!" he teased.

His daughter laughed. "I wish it was that easy."

Nancy phoned the police department and the post office. Nancy Smith Drew was not known at either place. Directories and telephone books gave no clue.

Nancy said good-by to her father and drove home. Bess and George were there, and were eager to hear the latest news. When Nancy gave them all the facts, the cousins gasped.

George remarked, "Things are certainly breaking fast. Now you have two mysteries on your hands. Well, tell us what we can do to help."

"Right now I don't have an idea in my head," Nancy confessed, "but I'll let you know."

She invited the girls to stay to dinner and they accepted at once. Mr. Drew had already told Hannah Gruen he would not be home until later so the four of them ate without him. They had just finished dessert when the doorbell rang.

"I'll get it," said Nancy.

When she opened the door a strange woman angrily forced her way inside and stepped toward the living room. The caller was poorly dressed in a worn-looking coat. Its collar was pulled up to her stringy, bleached hair.

"You're Nancy Drew, ain't you?"

When the girl nodded, the woman added, "You're the one I'm looking for!"

With that, her fist shot out and she tried to hit Nancy.

CHAPTER V

The Mysterious Gift

THOUGH taken unawares, Nancy managed to dodge the woman's blow. She grabbed the stranger's arm and held it firm.

"What are you trying to do?" she asked. "What do you want?"

"What I want are my rights!" the woman shouted.

"Who are you?" Nancy asked. She was sure she had never seen the woman before.

"I am Mrs. Skeets, and now that you've heard it you'll never forget it. And don't tell me you're not Nancy Drew, because I've seen you go running around town in that car of yours. I don't approve of young girls having cars. There are too many accidents as it is."

"Did you come here to lecture me about my driving?" Nancy asked the woman coldly.

"Certainly not. Anyway, I know it wouldn't do

no good. Girls today don't mind what their elders think. They go flyin' around as if they owned the earth."

"Will you please get to the point," Nancy interrupted her caller.

"Don't be pert, miss," Mrs. Skeets said. "I'll tell you in my own good time why I came here."

Nancy gritted her teeth. Was this woman unbalanced? She decided that perhaps if she did not answer, Mrs. Skeets would finally tell why she had come.

"Well, what you got to say about what you did?" the woman demanded.

Nancy heaved a sigh. "Mrs. Skeets, will you please tell me why you came here. I am not aware that I have ever met you or done anything to you."

"Well, to begin with, I'm Mrs. Maud Skeets. I'm Sailor Joe Skeets's wife, which is my bad luck. Never forgive him for forever sailin' off to all corners of the world and leavin' me to get along the best I can."

The woman took a deep breath before going on. "Joe's got a sister. She don't look like him and she don't act like him neither. One thing I must say, he ain't stingy. But that sister of his—all the money in the world and her not turnin' a finger, but the money just pourin' in because her husband invented some sort of stuff that takes stains out of cloth. Well, she condescends to send me ten dollars a week if you please. And where was last week's I ask you?" She stared hard at Nancy.

"I haven't the least idea," Nancy replied. "What makes you think I should know something about it?"

"Because my letter was in that bunch that was stolen from your house and you're to blame!" Mrs. Skeets almost screamed.

Nancy was amazed. She told the woman that she certainly was not to blame for the mail theft. "I never saw any of the letters that were taken. Perhaps yours wasn't among them."

"The day it was supposed to come was Saturday and one thing I will say about Joe's sister, she's always on time. No, that letter with the money in it was stolen!"

"I'm terribly sorry," said Nancy, "but as I said before I'm not to blame. Since there is nothing more to discuss I'll bid you good-by." She held the door open.

"Now see here, young lady, you aren't goin' to get rid of me that fast. You give me the ten dollars and I'll go."

Nancy's reply was firm. "I am not giving you ten dollars."

Mrs. Skeets tossed her head. "Uppity, eh?" she said. Then, seeing Bess, George, and Hannah Gruen who had come to the hall to see what the trouble was, she said sneeringly, "Reinforcements, eh? Well, that won't do you no good.

"You're to blame!" Mrs. Skeets screamed

You're just like all the other Nancy Drews."

"What do you mean?" Nancy demanded. "Have you known many?"

"Have I known many of them? Thank goodness, no!" Mrs. Skeets said, flinging her hands into the air. "Just you and the other one, and you're both cut out of the same cloth. Cheat people out of ten dollars and then pretend they're fine ladies and don't know nothin' about it."

Nancy asked Mrs. Skeets about the other Nancy Drew, but the woman refused to tell her anything.

"I'll make a bargain with you," she said. "You give me ten dollars and I'll tell you."

Nancy was wary that this might be a ruse of some kind and decided to try a few tactics of her own.

"If I change my mind, I'll come to see you tomorrow," she told Mrs. Skeets.

"Suits me." The woman grinned. "I'll bet you'll be around to see me. My house is 22 Cottage Street. It's not far from here, but it's not a grand neighborhood like yours. We're just plain folks over there."

With this cutting remark, she turned and went outside.

"Boy is she ever a weirdo!" George exclaimed.

Further discussion was interrupted by the telephone. Hannah Gruen picked it up, and in a moment said, "It's your father, Nancy, and he says it's important."

"I finally got an overseas call through to Mr. Bates-Jones," Mr. Drew said. "Nancy, the inheritance is sizable. He wants you to solve the mystery of the missing Nancy Drew!"

The girl chuckled. "Wonderful! Nothing I'd like better. And, Dad, I have a clue."

"What is it?"

She related the visit of the strange Mrs. Skeets, including the bargain to exchange information for the ten dollars. "Do you think I should do it?"

"Yes, I do."

"Then I'll go there tomorrow morning."

The following day, while Nancy was tidying up her room before leaving the house, Mrs. Gruen came in, holding a long evening dress over one arm.

"You haven't forgotten you're going to wear this Saturday evening, have you?" she teased.

"I'm afraid I had."

The housekeeper reminded her that the dress had to be shortened. "You'd break your neck in it at this length," she said. "Please put it on now and let me pin up the hem. Then I'll sew it while you're gone."

Nancy took off her skirt and sweater and slipped on the pale-blue evening dress. Glancing at herself in the mirror, she realized something was missing. Nancy studied herself as Hannah pinned up the skirt and kept telling her to turn a little at a time.

Suddenly Nancy realized what the costume needed—the lovely pearl necklace Mr. Drew had given her on her last birthday.

"The clasp is loose," she thought. "Before I go to Mrs. Skeets's house, I'll run down to the jeweler's with the necklace and have it fixed."

As soon as the housekeeper had finished pinning the hem, Nancy took off the dress. She put on her sports clothes once more, took the necklace from a drawer, and grabbed a coat.

"Wish me luck," she said, kissing Mrs. Gruen good-by. "I hope to bring home lots of news."

She drove directly to the center of town and parked. Mr. Whittier's jewelry shop was a block away. Nancy hurried down the street and entered the store.

"Good morning, Mr. Whittier," she said to the elderly man behind the counter. "I think the clasp on my pearl necklace needs tightening."

She took it from her purse.

The jeweler looked at it closely. "It certainly does," he said. "Are you in a hurry for it?"

Nancy told him she planned to take the necklace with her on Friday. "I'm going to Emerson for the weekend."

"Then I'll fix this right away."

As Mr. Whittier went to a room at the rear of the shop, he called out, "You caught me at a good time. I'm not particularly busy now. Make yourself comfortable."

While waiting, Nancy looked at the large assortment of rings, bracelets, pins, and other bits of jewelry in the display cases. How beautiful they all were!

Time passed quickly and soon the jeweler returned. He showed Nancy that the clasp worked perfectly now.

As he was wrapping it for her, Mr. Whittier said, "How did you like your beautiful new pin?"

"Pin?" Nancy repeated. "What pin?"

"The one that man got for you yesterday. He said he was going to give it to you right away."

Nancy was puzzled. What man was going to give her a pin?

CHAPTER VI

A Good Lead

"You look surprised," said Mr. Whittier. "I guess I gave away a secret."

"Oh, it's all right," Nancy assured him without divulging what was racing through her mind. The pin might be going to Nancy Smith Drew and here was her chance to find the heiress!

Nancy did not reveal her thoughts, however. Smiling, she said, "I must confess I haven't the least idea who might be giving me a pin, but it sounds exciting. I don't suppose you want to tell me who he is?"

The jeweler sighed. "I've told so much already I guess it won't matter. He said his name was Mr. Nixon and that he is from out of town."

Nancy was startled. Was he Edgar Nixon? Was he a friend of the heiress or of some other Nancy Drew?

·"Maybe Edgar Nixon *is* going to give the pin to

me, but there'll be some trick to it if he does," Nancy decided.

Mr. Whittier looked at her quizzically. "You seem kind of worried," he remarked. "I'm sorry I said anything. And please, when Mr. Nixon hands you the pin, don't let on I gave away a secret."

Nancy assured him she would not.

Suddenly she smiled. "If this man is the person I think he is, he's related to someone I know very well. Would you mind telling me what he looks like?"

"Well, he's kind of handsome you might say," Mr. Whittier replied. "Very thin and dark."

"What was he wearing?" Nancy asked.

She was not surprised to learn that the purchaser of the pin had worn a camel's-hair coat and hat. In her mind this settled it. The buyer was indeed Edgar Nixon. But where did she possibly fit into the picture?

Mr. Whittier handed Nancy the necklace. "Come in again soon," he invited her. "I'll have all my Christmas things on display next week."

His suggestion gave Nancy an idea. Recalling a remark her father had made, she said, "Mr. Whittier, in a magazine advertisement I saw a special kind of cuff links I know my dad would like. They were large gold squares and had diagonal stripes of black across them. I'd like a set to give Dad for Christmas."

"I know the pattern well," said Mr. Whittier. "I'll order a pair if you like."

"Please do, and let me know when they come in."

"Speaking of cuff links," said the jeweler, "Mr. Nixon bought a pair for himself. Kind of flashy but he seemed to like them. They were bright red and had a black star in the center."

Instantly Nancy thought what an excellent identification this was. Aloud she said, "I don't think I'd care for them myself."

Shortly thereafter, Nancy left the shop and walked to her convertible, deep in thought. She had just picked up two good leads!

Nancy went directly to the Skeets's home on Cottage Street. Although it was not far from the Drews', she had never been in this particular area. The houses were rather shabby, many of them needing paint, but they were neat and the windows glistened. The small lawns in front of them were well kept. Nancy drove slowly until she came to number twenty-two.

The bell knob on the seaman's cottage door was brightly polished. In answer to Nancy's ring, the door was opened by a grizzled, elderly man.

"Howdy," he said, smiling affably. "We don't want to subscribe to any magazines, thanky."

"I'm not selling anything." Nancy laughed. "I came to see Mrs. Skeets."

"Well, she hoisted anchor here about an hour ago," he said. "I expect she just rode around to the chandler for some supplies and most likely she'll be back by six bells."

Nancy grinned. "You mean eleven o'clock, Mr. Skeets?"

"Call me Sailor Joe like the rest of the folks." He grinned broadly. "Yes, miss. Six bells on a ship is 'leven o'clock."

"Then your wife will be back very soon," Nancy said, glancing at her wrist watch. "May I wait?"

"Heave your anchor, lass," Joe said. "Come into the parlor."

Chuckling, he led Nancy into the living room. It was papered in deep red and furnished in a variety of shabby furniture. On the walls were pictures of ships, a broken but highly polished sextant, a lethal-looking spear, and a large dried starfish.

Nancy sat down on a couch and remarked, "Sailing all over the world, you must have seen many interesting things, Mr. Skeets."

"Aye, and so I have." Sailor Joe grinned, settling himself in a captain's chair. "Why, a funny thing happened to me one time when I had shore leave in Melbourne, Australia. For fun I told one of the dockhands I was a pearl diver. And me not being able to swim a stroke. That night after

I'd gone to sleep, somebody came and carried me away. Next thing I knew I'd been shanghied onto a boat that was really going pearl diving."

Sailor Joe laughed uproariously. Nancy wondered what was so funny about this. Instead, it seemed tragic.

"I see you don't understand the joke," the old salt went on. "You see where I was brought up us sailors meant washin' dishes when we said pearl divin'." The old man rocked with laughter and slapped his knees with great calloused hands. Nancy laughed too but did not want Joe to get started on another one of his sea yarns. She was eager to ask him some questions before his wife returned.

"How long have you lived here?" she asked.

"Maybe a year, maybe two," Joe said. "My old woman moved out here so I'd be far from the sea and maybe stay home more. But I could smell salt water if I was in the middle of a desert! Speaking of deserts, I must tell you—"

Nancy interrupted quickly. "Did you ever know a young woman by the name of Nancy Drew?"

"Nancy Drew? Well, I'll say I did, and a trim little figurehead she was, and as neat as an admiral's cutter. Did you know her?"

Nancy shook her head. "I'm trying to locate a Nancy Smith Drew who's wanted in England," she said.

Sailor Joe whistled. "Wanted in England, is she? And for what? That girl never did a wrong thing in her life."

"Oh, she isn't wanted by the authorities," Nancy hastened to say. "A relative died and left her some money."

"Ah-ha! That's a jib of another cut." Joe grinned. "Yes, Nancy Smith Drew used to room with my missus in New York. She kept a roomin' house then.

"Well, well, I'm glad Miss Drew come into some money, for she was hard up, that she was. Studying for the stage, and a fine figure of an actress she'd 'a' made. Tall and beautiful with a fine deep voice."

Nancy was excited. "Where is Nancy Smith Drew now?"

Sailor Joe went on, "She couldn't get to sign with no theater, and at last she left us to go to some beach with a family as a governess."

Nancy was wildly elated at this clue. "When was this?" she asked.

"Oh, that was maybe ten—no, not that long. Let me see now. I remember I brought her back a souvenir and she was gone when I docked. What did I bring her? You'd never guess. A little monkey! I got it from a Portuguese—down in Brazil. I'd made a voyage to Rio in—Why, I remember now. It was just eight years ago next spring that Miss Drew left us."

Eight years ago! Nancy's heart sank.

"Do you remember the name of the family she went with?" she asked.

Sailor Joe pursed his lips and frowned. Presently he said, "English folks, I think. Name of Hilt something, or was it Washington? You know what? I gave that monkey to a man in exchange for a pair of boots."

As the old man burst into laughter again, Nancy felt more encouraged than ever, now that she had found another clue. Her thoughts were interrupted by an exclamation from Joe.

"Ahoy! Here comes the missus now. I know her step on the quarterdeck."

He jumped to his feet and rushed to open the door for Mrs. Skeets. Her arms were loaded with bundles.

"Brisket corned beef is what you'll get for supper because it's the cheapest cut in the market," the woman announced.

"Salt horse again!" exclaimed her husband. "Well, never mind. We got company."

Mrs. Skeets walked into the living room and saw Nancy. "Humph! It's you, is it!" She sniffed.

Without another word she passed through to the rear of the house and it was some minutes before the woman returned.

"Did you bring the money?" she asked.

"Hey, what's all this palaverin' about?" Joe demanded in annoyance.

"This is the young lady who's responsible for the disappearance of the letter from your sister that had ten dollars in it. I went around to her house. I suppose you've got the money with you?"

Joe looked from his wife to Nancy in bewilderment. "But this young lady didn't steal the money, did she?"

"I'm askin' no questions," Mrs. Skeets said stiffly. "All I want is our ten dollars."

Nancy smiled at Sailor Joe. "I'm glad you don't think I stole the money," she said. "Of course I didn't. A batch of letters was taken from our house, and your wife seems to think that a letter from your sister was among them."

"Well, I ain't goin' to let you pay one cent," Joe roared. "Not even a stevedore would agree to that."

"Nevertheless I made a bargain with your wife," Nancy told him. "I said I would give her the ten dollars in exchange for some information about Nancy Smith Drew."

"You see?" Mrs. Skeets said loftily. "Well, a bargain's a bargain. Let me see the ten dollars and then I'll talk."

Nancy took the money from her purse and held it up. She told the woman of the conversation that she had had with her husband. "I understand that Nancy Smith Drew was engaged as a governess by some English people several years ago."

"That's right, but Joe told you too much.

'Course this was a long time ago and I don't think it'll do you much good tryin' to find Nancy Smith Drew there. The name of the people was Wilson and they was stayin' at the Breakers Hotel somewhere on Cape Cod."

Nancy turned over the ten-dollar bill and started for the door. "Thank you both for the information. I shall try hard to find this other Nancy Drew. Mrs. Skeets, ask your husband to tell you about her inheritance."

As soon as Nancy reached home, she consulted the long-distance operator in order to dial the Breakers Hotel on Cape Cod. Finally she was given the number and put in the call. The man who answered said the place was closed for the winter. He was only the caretaker.

"I'm trying to locate people named Wilson who perhaps spend the summers there," Nancy said. "Could you give me their winter address?"

"No," the man replied. "I don't know the names of the summer guests and all the hotel's books are locked up. Maybe if you call next summer you can find out."

Nancy put down the phone and stared into space. Once more she had run into a stone wall. How should she proceed now?

As she sat lost in thought, the phone rang. She picked up the instrument and said, "Hello."

"Hi, Nancy!"

"Ned!"

"How's everything?" Ned Nickerson asked.

"You mean about the weekend? Just fine. Bess and George and I are driving up on Friday. We'll come right to Omega Chi Epsilon House. Okay?"

"That's what I was going to ask you to do. You girls will be staying here."

"Ned," Nancy said, "I'm busy solving two new mysteries."

She went on to give him a detailed account of Edgar Nixon, the stolen mail, and finally the mysterious letter which had come from England for Nancy Smith Drew.

At the end she laughed and said, "Of course I expect your help."

It was Ned's turn to chuckle. "I might be able to help you sooner than you think. You know there's to be a play Friday night—one of Shakespeare's. The dramatic society engaged a coach to come out from New York especially for it. She's a woman—and her name is N. Smith Drew!"

CHAPTER VII

The Wrecked Car

"Oh, Ned, do you mean it?" Nancy exclaimed. "Will you find out if the coach's first name is Nancy?"

He promised to do this and then added, "You'll be able to meet her Friday night. If she is Nancy Smith Drew, I won't tell her about the inheritance. I'll leave that for you."

Ned said he would call Nancy back as soon as he found out. "I won't leave the house until you do!" she told him.

It was an hour before Ned called back. "I didn't learn much," he reported. "Miss Drew was suddenly called away and she won't return until just before the show."

Nancy was disappointed but knew she must be patient. After all this was Wednesday. Friday evening was not too far away.

Ned changed the subject. With laughter in his voice, he said, "Who do you think is temporary coach? Burt Eddleton!"

Nancy giggled. George Fayne's date hardly seemed like the type to be coaching a Shakespearean play. He was a blond, husky football player who was full of fun.

"I can't wait," Nancy said. "Does Burt have a secret aspiration for becoming an actor after college?"

Ned laughed. "I doubt it."

The couple talked a few minutes longer, then they said good-by. Nancy's thoughts turned back to her visit at the Skeets's home and the information she had received.

Suddenly she told herself, "Maybe if N. Smith Drew, the coach, is Nancy Smith Drew from England, she went to see the Wilsons where she used to work as governess. If I could only find them!"

Nancy went upstairs. Hannah Gruen was still hemming the dance dress. Often when the girl sleuth was puzzled, she talked over the situation with the understanding housekeeper. Now she told her of the latest report from Ned Nickerson.

"I wish I knew where to find the Wilsons," Nancy said. "Have you any hunches?"

"If they summer in Cape Cod, possibly they live in the Boston area," was Mrs. Gruen's first guess.

"Yes," Nancy said slowly, "But lots of people

from other places go there too. What would be your second choice?"

"How about Springfield, Massachusetts?"

After a ten-minute conversation between them, Nancy came up with an idea which Mrs. Gruen thought was very plausible. Nancy Smith Drew had been in New York studying for the stage. If the N. Smith Drew at Emerson was the same person, she had no doubt succeeded in finding a place in the theatrical world—at least as a coach. There was a good possibility that the Wilsons, for whom she went to work as a governess, lived in New York City.

"I put a New York City phone book in your father's study," Mrs. Gruen told Nancy. "But I'll bet there are hundreds of people named Wilson in it."

Nancy hurried off. One look at all the Wilsons in New York City would have discouraged a less determined person. She took a pencil from her father's desk and began to check likely addresses.

She told herself that if the Wilsons could afford a governess, they were probably well-to-do. This meant they would live in one of the nice areas of the city. Consequently Nancy eliminated all the business and professional addresses. Her list of likely candidates turned out to be long, but she decided to start telephoning each one.

"Our phone bill will be tremendous," she told herself as call after call was made with no success.

Half an hour later Nancy heaved a sigh. Should she go on? Many things might have happened to the Wilsons she was trying to locate. They could have died or moved away.

"But I mustn't give up," Nancy told herself, and began to dial another number.

When a woman answered, Nancy said, "Is this Mrs. Wilson?"

"Yes."

"I'm making a long-distance call to you to ask a question. Did you ever employ a governess named Nancy Smith Drew?"

Nancy held her breath as she waited for the answer. "Who is calling?" the woman asked.

"Believe it or not, my name is also Nancy Drew. By chance I heard of Nancy Smith Drew and I'm trying to locate her. I received a letter by mistake which belongs to her."

There was a pause, then Mrs. Wilson said, "This is a great coincidence. Yes, a Miss Nancy Smith Drew worked for us a few years ago. She's a very lovely person and an excellent actress. Unfortunately I do not know where she is right now. Once in a while she sends us a postcard or a Christmas message. As a matter of fact, it has been almost a year since her last note, in which she said she was moving but did not give her future address."

Nancy was disappointed that the actress did not visit the Wilsons, but said, "I'm so thrilled to have located someone at last who knows Miss Drew. I must tell you what was in her letter. She has a large inheritance waiting for her in England."

"How exciting!" Mrs. Wilson exclaimed. "I'm so glad for her."

She and Nancy chatted for a few more minutes, then the woman said, "I'm sure I'll hear from Miss Drew at Christmastime. I'll tell her to get in touch with you at once. Where can she reach you?"

Nancy gave her address and telephone number and thanked Mrs. Wilson for her help. As soon as the conversation ended, Nancy went back to Hannah Gruen and told her the good news.

"Now I have two good leads. If the coach at Emerson is *not* Nancy Smith Drew, then by Christmastime we should hear from the right one."

Mrs. Gruen smiled. "I can see why you're a good detective," she remarked. "If you don't find hidden gold under one stone, you turn up another."

The housekeeper suggested that they take time out for lunch. After eating, the two returned to Nancy's bedroom to see if the evening dress was all right. Nancy kicked off her sports shoes, removed her skirt and sweater, then stepped into the dance dress. Hannah zipped it up.

Just then the phone rang and Nancy went into

her father's study to answer it. Chief McGinnis was calling.

"I thought you'd be interested to hear, Nancy, that we found the beat-up car with the license number TJ12796."

"You did?" Nancy exclaimed. "Where? And did you find Edgar Nixon too?"

"No, unfortunately." The officer explained that the car had been abandoned and was a complete wreck.

"We came across it on that road where you saw the man drive across the bridge," McGinnis added. "A little way beyond there was a sharp curve and I guess he was going too fast and didn't make it. But he evidently wasn't hurt much because he wasn't around and we've had no report from the hospital or any doctors about a person who needed attention."

"The car really did belong to Edgar Nixon?" Nancy asked.

"We don't know," McGinnis replied. "It was registered under another name with a phony address. Maybe the car was Nixon's, maybe a friend's."

"Or Edgar could be using aliases," Nancy thought.

The chief said if he had any further report he would telephone Nancy. "We're still looking for a man who wears a camel's-hair coat and hat, but we suspect that by this time he may have changed to something different."

"Perhaps," said Nancy. "But if he had a beat-up car and is demanding money from his brother Ira, I'd say he isn't very well off. Men's winter overcoats are expensive and I wonder if he could afford two of them."

Chief McGinnis laughed. "I admire the way your mind works, Nancy. What you just said is very true." He chuckled. "I guess we'll keep on looking for a man in a camel's-hair overcoat and hat."

As Nancy started back to her room so that Hannah Gruen could look at the dress, the front doorbell rang.

"I'll get it," Nancy called.

As she walked toward the stairway, Nancy realized that in her stocking feet the dress was pretty long. Just as she reached the top step, Nancy stepped on the front of the gown.

She heard a loud rip and gasped. At the same moment, she lost her balance and pitched forward!

CHAPTER VIII

Disheartening Request

As Nancy pitched forward she made a wild grab for the banister of the stairway. Though she swung around and almost lost her grip, Nancy managed to keep from falling.

"How stupid of me!" she chided herself, and went on down the stairway.

Nancy looked at the big rip in her lovely dress. Could it be mended without showing? "Oh, I hope Hannah can do something with it!"

She finally reached the bottom step and went on to the front door. When Nancy opened it, she was greeted by a grinning little boy.

"Hello," said Tommy Johnson.

"Hi, Tommy!" Nancy replied. "What are you holding behind your back?" she asked.

"A surprise," he said.

"For me?"

"Maybe. You know you promised me a 'tective badge for helping you."

"So I did," said Nancy. "Come in, Tommy. I'll get it for you right away."

Nancy hurried off to the dining room where there was a closet that held all sorts of knick-knacks. Among them was a toy detective badge which someone had given her at a party for a joke. She carried it to Tommy, who took it but still kept one hand behind his back.

"Do you like it?" Nancy asked.

"Sure I do. Would you put it on me, Nancy? After that, I'll show you what's in my other hand."

She pinned the badge onto his heavy sports jacket, then asked, "Have you brought me something exciting?"

"It's—what you say a clue," Tommy replied stoutly.

From behind his back he took out a man's rather worn shoe. Tommy explained that his little friend Billy down the street had picked it up.

"He saw it fall out of the yellow-coat man's car trunk," the little boy explained. "He just told me about it. I thought you might want the shoe, so I promised him some candy if he gave it to me. Do you have some candy?"

Nancy laughed and patted Tommy on the head. "Indeed I have and you shall have some as well as Billy. This is good detective work, Tommy. Keep it up and maybe someday you'll be a police chief."

"Oh boy, that would be something!" Tommy replied.

Nancy went to get two small jars of hard candy. She called them her emergency treats for just such occasions.

When she returned, Tommy's eyes expanded. "You mean I can have one whole jar, and Billy can have the other?"

Nancy nodded. "I think you both earned this reward."

Tommy went off, declaring that he was going to hunt for more clues to the yellow-coat man.

"I hope you don't catch him too soon," he called over his shoulder and Nancy giggled.

After she had closed the door, Nancy looked at the shoe thoroughly. She could see no identification of any sort. "But probably the police can find something," she thought. "I'll call Chief McGinnis and see what he has to say."

Fortunately he was in his office. "I'd say it's an excellent clue," he told her. "But don't bother to come down here now. Tomorrow will do."

Then Nancy climbed the stairs and showed Hannah the rip in her dress. The housekeeper said she was glad Nancy had not been hurt. She looked at the tear for some time.

"You really made a good job of this while you

were at it," she commented. "Well, take the dress off and I'll see what I can do with it."

Nancy said first she would slip on shoes with heels to see if the length of the dress was all right. She found it was, then took off the dress. Hannah turned it inside out.

"Good thing this rip is near a seam. It won't hurt to make the skirt a little narrower. I'll just put in a whole new seam."

"Oh, you are a darling!" Nancy said, and gave the housekeeper a kiss on the cheek.

Then she told Mrs. Gruen about the shoe. "It dropped out of the car that we think belonged to Edgar Nixon."

"Hm!" the housekeeper said. "I hope that shoe gets out of here in a hurry. I'm sure it's contaminated with bad luck."

"Why, Hannah, I've never heard you speak like that before."

"I can't help it," the housekeeper replied, starting to baste a new seam in the dress. "The man is no good, and I don't want any of his belongings around here."

When she finished sewing, Hannah laid the dress down and announced that she would have to start dinner. Nancy went downstairs to help her. She set the table and prepared a salad of tomatoes and cottage cheese.

"I won't put the steak on until your father comes," Mrs. Gruen remarked.

Nancy heard a step on the back porch. "I guess you can broil the steak now," she said, moving toward the door.

She opened it and her father entered. He kissed her, said good evening to the housekeeper, then beckoned for Nancy to follow him.

After he had hung up his coat and hat in the hall closet, he led the way into the living room. The two sat down.

"You have news?" Nancy queried.

"Yes. It's a mystery to me. Maybe you can figure it out. I had a cable late this afternoon from Mr. Bates-Jones."

The lawyer hesitated and Nancy sensed that what he was about to say was not going to please her. Finally he told her.

"You and I have been discharged," he said.

"Discharged from what?" Nancy asked.

"The Nancy Smith Drew Case."

"You mean they've found her?" Nancy cried, astonished.

Mr. Drew shook his head. "That's the mystery. The cable said someone else was putting them in touch with Nancy Smith Drew and that you and I could give up the case."

Nancy was amazed. "That's all the cable said?"

"Yes."

"Well, I think it's pretty abrupt when you have been so nice to make overseas phone calls to him."

Mr. Drew smiled. "Cables cost money. Perhaps

Mr. Bates-Jones will follow his message with a letter of explanation."

Nancy thought this over. Intuition told her that there was something quite unnatural about the whole thing.

"What's on your mind?" her father asked.

"Well, I think something phony is going on."

"You mean the cable?" her father asked.

"No. But I just have a strong hunch that there might be a fake Nancy Smith Drew posing as the real one."

The matter was discussed later with Hannah Gruen, who was inclined to agree with Nancy. "Call it woman's intuition if you like," she said. "If I were you, I wouldn't let it drop here."

"Perhaps you're right," Mr. Drew said. "I'll telephone to Mr. Bates-Jones in the morning and see if he will give me more details."

"May I be there when you make the call?" Nancy asked.

The lawyer smiled. "I'll make it from here before I leave for my office. I'd like you to hear what's said."

Directly after breakfast the following morning Mr. Drew put in the call to London. He had to wait several minutes before being connected with the lawyer there. Mr. Drew explained that he and Nancy did not want to go against Mr. Bates-Jones's wishes, but were calling to find out if the real Nancy Smith Drew had been located.

"We have some good leads to her ourselves," Nancy's father said, "so your cable was a great surprise."

Nancy, who was seated near the phone, could hear the answer plainly.

"We appreciate your great interest and all the trouble you have gone to," Mr. Bates-Jones said, "but we have had a communication from an American detective agency that for a fee they will tell us the secret whereabouts of the heiress."

Mr. Drew frowned. "But how did they learn you're looking for her?"

"That we don't know, but we have no reason to believe the firm is not telling the truth."

"Perhaps I could be of help to you," Mr. Drew said, "by looking up this agency. It's just possible that a thorough investigation might be to your advantage."

There was a long pause. "Well," the London lawyer finally said, "I think it best not to divulge the name."

Nancy and her father looked at each other. This certainly was a brush-off!

Before saying good-by, Mr. Drew added, "Frankly, Mr. Bates-Jones, my daughter and I are very suspicious about this. I advise you not to part with any money until the whole thing has been thoroughly investigated."

There was a loud exclamation at the other end of the wire. Finally the London attorney said,

"Thank you for your advice, Mr. Drew. I will talk to my partner about the case and let you know the result."

When the conversation had ended, Mr. Drew said he must hurry off. After he had gone, Nancy settled down in a big chair to think. Intuition told her she must not give up the case. Yet what else could she do?

Suddenly she remembered something and thought, "I still have another case—Edgar Nixon and the money stolen from Dad's registered letter. I can work on that."

CHAPTER IX

"He's Not a Suspect!"

THE ringing of the telephone brought Nancy out of her meditation. The caller was Ira Nixon. He sounded very weak.

"Is something the matter?" Nancy asked quickly, fearful that the mail carrier had taken a turn for the worse.

"Will you please come over right away?" the old man asked.

Nancy promised to leave immediately. She went to the kitchen to tell Mrs. Gruen where she was going.

"I hope he isn't worse," the housekeeper said. "The poor fellow's probably starved. Nancy, I want you to take him a jar of the fresh vegetable soup I prepared for tonight's dinner."

"I'll be happy to," Nancy said.

Hannah ladled some of the soup into a jar. She

then put it in a paper bag, but before handing the package to Nancy, she said, "And don't forget to take that old shoe out of here."

Nancy laughed. "It's going to police headquarters as fast as I can get it there. But I must go to Ira's first."

Fifteen minutes later she arrived at Ira Nixon's little white house. The front door was unlocked and she let herself in. The mail carrier, haggard and worried-looking, sat in a rocker near the fireplace. He explained that he had had a chill and one of his neighbors had come in to build a fire.

"Everybody is so kind to me except—except my brother. He gives me orders every time he comes here."

Nancy sat down. "Did he come to get money from you?"

Ira Nixon shook his head. "Not this time," he said. "And that's why I sent for you. Here's what happened.

"Edgar came here about an hour ago. As soon as he'd gone I tried to get you on the phone but it was busy. My brother was all dressed up as usual and he has a new car. It's red."

Nancy made no comment about the new car, but she was thinking hard. "Yes?" she urged Mr. Nixon, who had stopped speaking. "Go on."

"Nancy, that boy had nothing to do with my hard luck, I'm sure of that now." The postman continued. "He said he came here as soon as he heard about the mail robbery. He was as sympathetic as you are. Wanted me to give him some of my inheritance to hire a private detective and clear up the whole matter."

"Have you received all of your inheritance?" Nancy asked.

"Not a cent. I told him that."

Ira Nixon went on to say that Edgar had tried to talk him into handing over any money he had on hand. "He said he would take care of all the details of hiring a detective, but some cash would help a lot."

Nancy had her own idea of just how much detective hiring Ira would have received for the money, but she said nothing.

"So you see," Ira continued, "you were all wrong about Edgar. He's not a suspect. He knew nothing about the stolen mail. He's too dictatorial to suit me, but I certainly can't say he's a thief."

Nancy made no comment but asked, "Did your brother happen to say where he's staying?"

"Oh yes. There's no secret about that," Mr. Nixon went on. "He's boarding up in Ridgefield. He even gave me his address. I have it written down here. Wait a minute—

"Here it is!" Ira took a slip of paper from the pocket of his bathrobe. "He boards with a family named Hemmer on Harrison Street."

Nancy got up to leave. "By the way, did your brother ever mention a girl friend?"

"Not until today," the old man replied. "Edgar said he's going to marry a rich girl very soon."

"What's her name?"

"He didn't say."

Nancy wondered if it could be the English Nancy Drew. In any case, she decided to go to Ridgefield right away and see what she could find out. Before leaving, Nancy asked if Edgar Nixon were employed.

His brother shrugged. "We never discussed his affairs. He was always well dressed and had a car, so I guess he made a good living."

Further suspicion ran through Nancy's mind. It seemed most unnatural for a brother to be so uncommunicative. It was just possible that Edgar's way of earning a living was too shady for him to reveal.

After saying good-by to Ira Nixon, Nancy drove directly to police headquarters and asked to see Chief McGinnis. She was told to go right into his office.

"Hello, Nancy," he said. "You've been neglecting us lately." He grinned and added, "I thought you'd have the mystery of the missing mail solved by this time."

"Not quite yet," Nancy replied. "But I do have some interesting clues. Here's one of them," she

"Here's one of the clues," said Nancy

said, handing over the worn shoe to Chief Mc-
Ginnis.

Nancy went on to bring the chief up to date
about all the information she had on the suspect.

"I'm going to drive up to Ridgefield and do a
little investigating," she said. "If I turn up any
valuable clues, shall I get in touch with you or
the Ridgefield police?"

"You'd better tell the chief up there."

Directly after lunch Nancy phoned Bess and
George and asked if they could drive over to
Ridgefield with her. George said at once she
would not miss it for anything.

"Is this a dangerous assignment?" Bess queried.

Nancy laughed. "I haven't heard yet that Edgar
Nixon gets rough, but then you never can tell."

At once Bess knew she was being teased. "I'm
not chicken. When do you want me to be ready?"

"In half an hour. Okay?"

"I guess I could put on some lipstick and
powder and get my hair combed by that time,"
Bess replied.

Before leaving, Nancy called her father to see
if any further word had come from England. She
was told No.

"I guess we'll just have to wait for a letter," the
lawyer said.

Nancy then told him of her proposed trip to
Ridgefield and the new clues she had picked up.

"Good for you," her father said. "Well, I hope

the next time I talk to my daughter, she'll have lots of good news for me."

"I'll try hard."

A few minutes later Nancy set off. She picked up George first and then went on to the Marvin home. Bess was not waiting for her in front of the house so Nancy honked the horn. Her friend did not appear.

A look of disgust came over George's face. "That cousin of mine never watches the clock. She's probably writing letters and making phone calls and doing a lot of things and here we are waiting."

Nancy tooted again. When Bess still did not come outside, she got out of the car and went to the front door.

At that instant Bess opened it. She apologized for being late and said she had just finished talking to Dave Evans, who had called her from Emerson.

"I have something interesting to tell you, Nancy," she said. "Ned tried to phone you but you'd already left the house. I'm glad Dave caught me."

"What is the big news?" Nancy asked, trying not to be impatient.

Bess explained that the young woman who was coaching the Shakespearean play and was known as N. Smith Drew was indeed Nancy Smith Drew.

"How marvelous!" Nancy exclaimed.

"There's more to it," Bess went on.

As the two girls reached Nancy's convertible, she related the first part of the message to George. Then she added, "Nancy Smith Drew has gone to Ridgefield!"

"Ridgefield?" Nancy cried out.

The three girls stared at one another, the same thought flashing through their minds. Was it merely coincidence that the actress and Edgar Nixon had gone to Ridgefield at the same time? Or had she perhaps been drawn into some kind of racket with the suspect?

Bess exclaimed, "Wouldn't that be awful!"

George expressed a further thought. "Maybe Miss Drew found out he stole the letter from England and went to Ridgefield to get it."

Bess looked puzzled. "Are you trying to say Edgar plans to keep her from learning about the inheritance?"

"Could be," George answered. "I wouldn't put anything past that man."

Nancy nodded. All the suspicions she had had about Edgar Nixon now came back to her.

"Of course all this doesn't explain the money sent to Dad which was stolen," she said.

"Edgar's a slick one," George remarked.

Nancy was worried. "Girls, I'm afraid that he intends to marry Nancy Smith Drew, perhaps in Ridgefield, and enjoy the inheritance that is coming to her."

"How despicable!" Bess cried. "And Miss Drew, I'm sure, is too nice a person to be tied to a dishonest husband."

George grinned. "In any case, we'd better get to Ridgefield as fast as we can and stop the wedding!"

CHAPTER X

Search for a Bride

"It's starting to snow," Bess remarked as a few flakes hit the windshield of Nancy's convertible.

Before leaving home, she had put the top up because the day was cloudy and raw, with a hint of stormy weather.

Bess went on, "Oh, I hope it won't be bad. Nancy, does this car have snow tires?"

Before Nancy could reply, George spoke up. "Bess, you have so little faith in people. Of course Nancy would have snow tires and good ones at that."

Her cousin defended herself quickly. "After working with Nancy on all the mysteries she's asked us to help her solve, you know even the smartest people can be forgetful sometimes!"

Nancy laughed. "You girls have driven with me in snowstorms many times. Nevertheless I promise to be careful. Oh, it's getting to be worse fast."

Due to the storm, it took longer to get to Ridgefield than Nancy had hoped, but she was buoyed up by an exciting thought. Soon she would either come face to face with Edgar Nixon or find out whether or not he was married.

When the girls arrived on the outskirts of Ridgefield, the snow was deep. Nancy asked directions to Harrison Street. She found it blocked off by a snow removal machine which had stalled.

Nancy turned down a hill and parked near the foot of it. The three girls climbed back up, turned right on Harrison Street, and trudged along the unshoveled sidewalk.

Finally they came to Mrs. Hemmer's guesthouse. By this time the girls were covered with snow. Before stepping onto the porch, they brushed off what snow they could and stamped their boots.

Nancy rang the bell. In a minute it was answered by a plain-looking woman in her sixties. She looked surprised to see the three callers.

"What can I do for you?" she asked. "You lost or just cold?"

The girls smiled and Nancy replied, "We're all right. We had to park on the next street so we got covered with snow walking up here. Is Mr. Edgar Nixon at home?"

"Why—uh—no," Mrs. Hemmer answered. "What do you want to see him about?"

"When will he be back?" Nancy replied, deliberately evading the woman's question. Mrs. Hemmer surveyed her callers from head to toe before saying, "You look like nice honest young ladies. The answer is that Edgar Nixon moved out this morning."

"Oh!" the three girls chorused.

"Did you know ahead of time he was going?" Nancy queried.

"No, I didn't," the woman said. "He never hinted at such a thing. As a matter of fact, he seemed quite happy here. But then, I suppose when you inherit money you want to move to better quarters."

The girls tried not to show their excitement at this statement. Nancy said nonchalantly, "So Edgar inherited some money?"

Mrs. Hemmer became more talkative. "It's kind of cold for me standin' here. Won't you come inside?"

Nancy and her friends followed the woman. She led them to her living room, which was cheerful despite the dull day.

"Mr. Nixon didn't say where the money was coming from," Mrs. Hemmer went on, "but he told me it was a big sum and now he was going to change his type of work."

"What sort of work did he do?" George asked.

"That I don't know," the woman replied. "Mr. Nixon was kind of mysterious about his affairs, but I suspect he was in some mail-order business. He received lots of letters."

Nancy could see her excellent clue fast petering out. No doubt Edgar would have notified the post office already of his change of address. Finally Nancy asked the question that was uppermost in her mind.

"Did Edgar Nixon say he was going to be married, Mrs. Hemmer?"

"Not this morning he didn't," the woman said. "But he mentioned it yesterday."

"I suppose he was pretty excited about it," Nancy remarked, trying hard not to show her rising excitement. "Who's the young lady?"

Mrs. Hemmer said he had not mentioned her name. "But I suppose she was the one who came here this morning."

The three girls looked at one another. Before they had a chance to ask anything about her, Mrs. Hemmer went on, "To tell you the truth, I don't think it was very polite of Mr. Nixon not to introduce her to me. I went to the door and let her in. He came rushing down the stairs with his two suitcases and said, 'Let's go!' "

Nancy heaved a sigh, but tried not to reveal her great disappointment. "I'm sure she's the person we're trying to find. Too bad you didn't learn her name. Can you tell us anything about her?"

"I didn't pay particular attention," Mrs. Hemmer answered. "She was tall and all bundled up in fur. I did notice, though, that she spoke with a British accent."

Now there was no doubt in Nancy's mind that the person who had come to the house was Nancy Smith Drew. Her heart sank as she thought that by this time she and Edgar Nixon might be husband and wife.

"We must go," Nancy said. "Thank you for all the time you've given us." She smiled. "Don't be surprised if we come back and call on you again."

"Glad to see you any time," the woman told her.

As the girls trudged up the snowy street, Bess said, "Do you plan to do any more sleuthing in Ridgefield?"

"I'm going to the Town Hall and see if Edgar Nixon took out a marriage license," Nancy told her.

Through inquiries she learned that the building was not far away, so the girls decided to walk there. They were told that no marriage license had been issued to the couple.

"They could have been married almost any place," Bess spoke up. "Trying to get that information would be like hunting for a needle in a haystack."

Nancy turned back to the clerk and said, "Do you have a justice of the peace in this town?"

"Yes we do. He has an office on the second floor."

Nancy thanked the clerk and motioned for the girls to follow her up the stairs. The justice of the peace was a short, rotund man with a jolly look. He seemed amused by Nancy's inquiry. She guessed that he was thinking, "This girl's disappointed about losing her fiancé and is trying to find out about his elopement with someone else!"

"I haven't married anybody for a month," the justice of the peace said, "and never anyone named Edgar Nixon or Nancy Drew."

He suggested that one of the clergymen in town might have performed the ceremony. "Suppose I give you a list," he said, "and you can go around and find out for yourself."

He opened a drawer and pulled out a pad. In a few moments he had written out a rather long list.

"I appreciate this," Nancy said. "Because of the storm I don't think I'll try visiting all these people."

The justice of the peace told her there was a pay telephone booth in the main lobby of the building. "You'll keep drier if you try calling up, instead of going out in the snow."

Nancy agreed, thanked the man for his help, and went downstairs with the girls. They pooled their coins and took turns dialing the names on the list. Fortunately all the men were at home, but said that they had not performed any marriage ceremony for a couple of weeks. Furthermore, they had had no requests for any during the next week.

When Nancy completed the last call, Bess remarked, "Nancy, you look pretty downcast. This trip in the snow is all for nothing."

George tried to cheer up her friend. "I have a suggestion. Why don't we go back to Mrs. Hemmer's and ask if she would mind our looking for clues in Edgar's room?"

Nancy thought it was an excellent idea and once more the girls plowed through the snowy streets to the guesthouse.

"You're back?" the woman remarked. "Wouldn't your car start?"

"To tell the truth, I haven't tried it," Nancy answered. "Mrs. Hemmer, it's very important that I locate Edgar Nixon as soon as possible. We girls thought possibly he left some clue to his whereabouts in his room."

"I don't mind you looking around one bit," the woman said. "As a matter of fact, I'm very glad you came back. Several registered letters came in for Mr. Nixon right after you left. Out of force of habit I signed for them. After the mail carrier left, I realize that I didn't know where to send the letters. Then I suddenly remembered something. Did you tell me before that your name is Nancy Drew and that you come from River Heights?"

"That's right."

"Did you ever hear of a man named Ira Nixon who lives there?"

Nancy smiled. "He's our mail carrier. As a matter of fact he's a brother of Edgar."

"I know that," Mrs. Hemmer said. "Maybe you could help me out with these letters. Some time ago Mr. Nixon said to me, 'In case of an emergency, get in touch with my brother Ira in River Heights.' "

The three girls were watching Mrs. Hemmer intently. What would she reveal next?

The woman went on, "If you could just prove to me that you're Nancy Drew from River Heights I'd give you these letters to take to his brother."

Nancy showed her driver's license, but said, "Suppose I give you Ira Nixon's telephone number, you can dial it and tell him I'm here."

The woman asked Nancy to make the call and she would talk with Ira Nixon. After a short delay Ira Nixon came on the line. Nancy identified herself, told where she was, and introduced Mrs. Hemmer.

"You take it now," she said, handing the woman the phone.

Mrs. Hemmer told him the story and he verified the fact that Nancy was really Nancy Drew from River Heights and that he had known her since she was a little girl.

"Your brother Edgar has moved away from here," she said. "He told me that in an emergency I should get in touch with you. I think these letters should be turned over to you. Shall I give them to Nancy Drew?"

"By all means," the girls heard him reply. "Nancy Drew is one of the most reliable persons I've ever met and she's trying to help me solve a mystery. Mrs. Hemmer," he asked suddenly, "you never had any reason to think my brother isn't perfectly honest?"

"Oh no," the woman answered. "He always paid his rent on time and came and went without any trouble to me. Of course he never told me much about himself, but then it's just as well not to have too much talk between a guesthouse owner and her roomers."

The bundle of letters proved to be too big for Nancy's purse or even coat pocket. Since it had stopped snowing, she decided it would be all right for her to carry them in her hand as far as the car.

Before leaving, the three girls searched Edgar's room but found no clues to where he had gone. Finally they said good-by to Mrs. Hemmer and hurried down Harrison Street. When they reached the street on which the convertible was parked, Bess suggested it would be easier to walk down the hill in the middle of the street rather than on the sidewalk.

They had hardly started when a boy on a sled whizzed around the corner. The next second he skidded into Nancy.

The impact knocked her sprawling into the snow. The bundle of letters flew from her hand and scattered in every direction.

CHAPTER XI

The Strange Messages

BESS and George rushed to Nancy's aid. They helped her up and asked solicitously if she were hurt.

Nancy smiled ruefully. "Mostly my feelings," she said with a wry smile. "My leg does hurt a little, though. I'd like to sit down."

The girls assisted her to the porch of a house where the steps had been cleared of snow. Nancy sat down and rubbed the bruise on her leg.

Bess and George looked at each other. Nancy was very white and they kept asking her over and over again how she really felt and should they take her to a doctor.

"Oh no!" she replied. "I'll be all right in a minute. You girls had better go pick up those letters. They're getting soaked in the snow."

As the cousins started for the street, several children on sleds came speeding down the hill.

They ran over the letters, burying them deeper and mutilating them. Bess and George hurried to pick them up.

The girls returned to the porch and Nancy stared at the letters in dismay. Some of them were open, others were torn and two had the contents sticking out.

"Oh look!" George exclaimed. "This letter has money in it. Wow! Twenty-five dollars!"

She handed the envelope to Nancy, who immediately looked for a return address. There was none. "Maybe there's one on the letter inside," she suggested.

"I'm going to look and see," Bess declared, and began to read the already-opened letter. In a moment a broad grin spread across her face. "Listen to this:

'Dear Guide,
I am so excited at the thought that I am soon to meet the man of my dreams. I can hardly work. Please don't keep me waiting.

Mildred' "

Now Bess's amusement turned to a serious mood. "We might be all wrong about Nancy Smith Drew," she said. "Maybe Edgar is going to marry this person Mildred."

"Is there an address on the letter?" Nancy asked.

"No."

George remarked, "What puzzles me is why

twenty-five dollars is in the letter. Pretty soft, if Edgar can get twenty-five dollars out of his future bride!"

"Where was the letter mailed?" Nancy asked.

"Dorset."

Bess looked at Nancy. "You think maybe Edgar went to Dorset to marry Mildred?"

Nancy smiled. "Perhaps. Are there any more open letters with money in them?"

George looked through the dirty, rumpled mail. "Yes, here's another. And there's twenty-five dollars in it!"

Nancy asked her to read the letter, saying, "I'm beginning to be suspicious of something. I'll tell you in a minute."

"'Dear Guide:
I am so thrilled! It won't be long before I'll be in the arms of the man fate has sent me! I am counting the hours!

Martha'"

There was no return address on either the letter or the envelope.

"What is your suspicion, Nancy?" Bess asked.

"That Edgar Nixon is a bigamist—or even a tri-gamist?"

"More likely," George put in, "he promises, for sums of money, to marry a whole bunch of women, and when things get too hot, he just skips out. This time, with Nancy learning too much about him, he had to leave before he had a chance to pick up the last bunch of letters. I'll bet there's twenty-five dollars in every one of these!"

"Shall we find out?" Bess asked eagerly.

Nancy shook her head. "To read an open or half-open letter is one thing. But to open the whole thing and snoop inside is illegal."

"Nancy, you haven't told us your theory yet," George reminded her.

The girl detective laughed. She said teasingly, "I haven't had a chance! I suspect that Edgar Nixon has been running a Lonely Hearts Club and gets money for promising to find a husband, or a wife, for the person who is foolish enough to put his or her trust in Edgar."

George snorted. "Do you think the silly people believe they are going to get a mate for twenty-five dollars?"

"Oh no," Nancy replied. "I would judge that the whole thing is done on an installment plan. These two letters which we have read are probably the last installment."

"So that's why Edgar had to skip out!" Bess suggested, and Nancy nodded.

"The scheme is positively revolting!" George exclaimed.

"And more than that," Bess said, "it's heartbreaking. A Lonely Hearts Club turned into a Hopeless Hearts Club."

George had several uncomplimentary things to

say about Edgar Nixon. Then suddenly she paused in the middle of a sentence. Her eyes flashed. "Do you suppose Nancy Smith Drew is one of Edgar's victims?"

Bess said, "If she is, and he didn't intend to marry her, why did Edgar let her come here?"

Nancy looked thoughtful. "I still think he intends to marry her. He knows about the inheritance, but she doesn't, and he isn't going to let her find out until after they're married. Then, through some clever scheme, he plans to get the money away from her."

"We mustn't let him do that!" Bess cried.

George looked hard at her cousin. "And just how can we stop him? We don't know where he is. Miss Drew came here and went away with him and—"

"And what else?" Bess asked her, a bit miffed by George's gruffness.

Her cousin did not answer, but said, "Nancy, what do you intend to do with these letters? Are you still going to take them to Ira Nixon?"

Nancy shook her head. "I don't think that would be wise. In the first place, the poor old man would probably collapse again. I'd hate to be responsible for that. If his brother is a swindler, I feel that the authorities should inform Ira, not me."

The other girls agreed.

"I think we should go at once to the postmaster here and explain everything."

"Will you tell him your suspicions about the Lonely Hearts Club?" Bess questioned.

"I think I will," Nancy answered. "Even if I'm wrong, it won't hurt for the post office to make an investigation. Men don't just disappear without leaving any forwarding address unless they have something to hide."

Nancy declared that she felt much better now. She got up and trudged down the hill with the girls to her car. She inquired from some children where the post office was and drove directly there. Unfortunately the building was closed.

"Now what?" George asked. "Don't tell me we have to stay in this town all night!"

Bess grinned. "I'm sure Mrs. Hemmer would be glad to accommodate us in Edgar's vacated room."

The other girls laughed, then Nancy replied, "Since the letters were entrusted to my care, I'll take them home and tomorrow morning take them to the River Heights post office."

It was late by the time the girls reached River Heights. Nancy took her friends home, then started for her own house. She was eager to tell her father and Hannah Gruen the latest developments in the mystery.

Nancy was mulling over the case as she turned

into the Drews' driveway. One thing was a complete puzzle—the part about the American detective agency getting in touch with Malmsbury and Bates-Jones in London.

She put the car away and walked slowly toward the kitchen door. Just before she reached it, a startling idea came to her. Could Edgar Nixon, to throw suspicion from himself, have gone to a shady detective agency and said he knew where the missing Nancy Smith Drew was? He could have asked them to contact Malmsbury and Bates-Jones. Then his own unsavory schemes would never be suspected.

CHAPTER XII

A Fresh Puzzle

MR. DREW was waiting for Nancy in the kitchen and she thought she detected relief in his expression.

"Dad, were you worried about me?"

"I certainly was. The storm didn't hit us very much, but I heard on the radio it was heavy over in Ridgefield."

"It was, and this accounts for a few adventures I had," she said.

Hannah Gruen, vigorously whipping potatoes in a pot, turned with questioning eyes. "Were you in an accident with the car? Did you get hurt?"

"Only a little accident, but not with the car. I have a few bruises on one leg where a boy on a sled ran into me. Don't worry," she added, as the housekeeper stopped her dinner preparations and came over to examine the injury.

"If it hadn't been for the sled, the letters

wouldn't have opened and we wouldn't have found the money in them nor known that Edgar Nixon is probably running a Lonely Hearts Club—"

Mr. Drew held up his hand to interrupt. "For Pete's sake, Nancy," he said, "please take off your heavy clothes and we'll sit down at the table. Then you can tell your story from beginning to end. It sounds interesting."

Mrs. Gruen had prepared a delicious roast beef dinner, which they all enjoyed. During the meal, Nancy told about her adventures. The others were amazed and agreed that no doubt her conclusions about Edgar Nixon were correct.

Mr. Drew approved the idea of the letters being taken to their local postal inspector first thing in the morning. "But you'll have to tell Ira. Suppose you say how the letters got damaged and you thought the post office should have them."

"All right, Dad. That should satisfy him. I certainly don't want to hurt poor Ira at this time."

Nancy asked her father if any further word had come from Mr. Bates-Jones in London. Her father shook his head.

"In a way," Mr. Drew added, "I'm glad there is no news. Tomorrow you and Bess and George go to Emerson, don't you?"

"Yes, Dad. I expect it will be an exciting weekend."

"Well, I want you to enjoy it and not have the mystery on your mind. There is something in the evening paper that I think will interest you," Mr. Drew added as they all rose from the table.

He went to get the newspaper and turned to the sports section. He pointed out a headline, which made Nancy's heart skip a beat. It said:

EMERSON COUNTS ON NICKERSON TOE

The article went on to tell of Ned's prowess at punting and kicking field goals. Nancy felt very proud to be his guest.

"It ought to be a great game," Mr. Drew remarked. "Wish I could be there, but you'll have to tell me all about it Monday."

The lawyer went for his coat and said he was going out to bowl with some friends. After he had gone, Nancy started to help Hannah tidy the dining room and kitchen, but the housekeeper urged her to go upstairs and pack.

"There's not much to do here," she told Nancy. "You'll have to get up early if you're going to stop at the post office, and then pick up George and Bess. It's a long drive to Emerson and you'll want time to change your clothes before the play. It's tomorrow night, isn't it?"

"Yes, and I hope to meet Nancy Smith Drew face to face. You know, Hannah, it is just possible that Edgar Nixon may have gone to Emerson with her. Oh, I only hope that they won't

be married before they get there and I can try
to prevent the wedding."

Nancy had just started her packing when she
heard the doorbell ring. In a few seconds she became aware that the housekeeper was arguing
with someone. Then Hannah Gruen climbed the
stairs and poked her head into the doorway of
Nancy's room.

"It's that pest again," she said with a sigh. "I
told her to go away, because you were very busy,
but she's insistent and won't budge until she has
seen you."

Nancy smiled. "You mean Mrs. Skeets?"

"Yes. What will I tell her?"

"I guess I'd better talk to her," Nancy said.
"You may never get rid of her if I don't find out
what she wants."

Nancy walked down to the front hall where
Mrs. Skeets was standing. The woman was well
bundled up, but her stringy hair showed below
her hat.

"I knew you'd see me," she crowed as Nancy
appeared.

"What can I do for you?" Nancy queried.

"As I told you once before, I don't want nothin' except what's mine," Mrs. Skeets said.

Nancy suspected the woman was going to ask
for additional money and said quickly, "Don't expect anything more from me."

"Now, young lady," Mrs. Skeets retorted, shaking a finger at Nancy, "don't get uppity with me or you may regret it. I came here on an errand of good will, I want you to know. But if you don't show proper respect for your elders—and what young folks do these days, I ask you—I'll go away and you'll never learn why I came."

Nancy was amused by this tirade, but also curious to know what the errand of good will was.

"I'm listening."

"Well, that's good. Most o' the girls today won't listen to their elders. Nope, I'd say the chicks seem to think they can teach the old birds to fly." Mrs. Skeets laughed loudly at her own joke. "As I've said more than once to Mrs. Brant next door, who has eight young uns, 'Mrs. Brant, I said—' "

Nancy interrupted. "Please tell me why you really came here. I am very busy upstairs."

Mrs. Skeets frowned in an annoyed way, then said, "Well, I came to tell you all the missin' letters was mailed back to their owners."

Nancy was so surprised she stepped backward. The idea of such a thing happening after all this time left her speechless for the moment.

"Ah-ha, I thought that would knock you over!" Mrs. Skeets exclaimed. "Now maybe you'll listen to me."

Nancy realized that the letters stolen from the

Drews had not been returned. She said, "How do you know all the letters were mailed back to the people?"

" 'Cause I went around and asked everybody in the neighborhood. It all started this way. We got a new mail carrier. This mornin' he came to our door and handed me three letters. The first one I looked at was the electric bill, which was away too high. We're folks for early sleepin', and I never ran no eight dollars' worth of electric last month and the company is goin' to hear from me, you can bet."

Nancy repressed a smile as Mrs. Skeets went on, "The next letter wasn't a letter at all, but a postcard from an old neighbor of mine in New York, only she lives in Florida now.

"She bought a house down there several years ago. Looked good then but it's fallin' apart, and ain't worth half what she paid for it. But she hasn't any money, so she lives in it, and she says what the rich people find in Florida she can't—"

"Oh, Mrs. Skeets, please," Nancy cried in exasperation. "What has all this to do with your being here to see me?"

"I'm comin' to that," Mrs. Skeets said. "Just give me time. As I was sayin'—where was I now? See, you made me forget!

"Oh yes. The other letter, mind you, was from Joe's sister. And I knew right well she wouldn't write twice a week even if someone held her hand

to guide the pen. And there was the ten dollars
in the letter too, and she wouldn't send me
twenty dollars in one week any more'n she'd send
me a million. So I got an idea and looked at
the postmark. Sure enough, just as I suspected,
it was stamped twice by the post office here!"

"This will make Ira Nixon very happy," Nancy
remarked.

The woman pulled ten dollars from her pocket. "I suppose I owe you an apology, but any-
how here's your ten dollars."

"Thank you very much," said Nancy. "I'm re-
lieved the whole matter is straightened out."

She was glad Mrs. Skeets had not asked her
whether the Drew mail had also been returned. It
would only have led to another long speech.

The sailor's wife put her hand on the doorknob,
but before turning it, she looked straight at
Nancy and with a smirk said, "I guess you've had
your fun."

"What do you mean?" Nancy demanded.

Mrs. Skeets gave a raucous laugh. "Oh, I can
see how two or three young girls in this day and
age might think it funny to steal a poor old mail
carrier's letters and hide the whole lot of 'em
from the rightful owners for a day or two. I'm
not so blind I can't see through a knothole."

Nancy was furious. "Mrs. Skeets, you have no
right to insinuate such a thing. Neither I nor
my friends would be guilty of such a low trick!

And the post office wouldn't think it was any joke. We'd be liable."

"Maybe so, maybe so," said Mrs. Skeets. She opened the front door with a flourish and stepped onto the porch. "I can't help havin' my thoughts, though. But I won't say anything. Don't think I'm a gossip. Good-by!" She went down the front steps.

By this time Hannah Gruen had joined Nancy. As the suspicious woman walked out of sight down the driveway, the housekeeper remarked:

"Imagine having to live with such a person! I don't blame Sailor Joe for taking long voyages to get away from her!"

Nancy burst into laughter, then reminded Mrs. Gruen that the Drews' letters had not been returned.

"I suspect that the thief had planned to steal only our mail but didn't have much time and so he took everything. He couldn't guess there was money in Mrs. Skeets's letter and he wasn't interested in the contents of any others except ours."

Mrs. Gruen nodded. "This directly involves you in the case. Well, honey, you'd better get back to your packing."

Nancy had just finished when Mr. Drew returned. He laughed heartily at her story of Mrs. Skeets and then said he thought Nancy's theories about the stolen letters were correct.

"This seems to pinpoint the fact that the mail

thief, who is probably Edgar Nixon, was after the letter to my client which had a large sum of money in it. Whether or not he knew about the message for Nancy Smith Drew is something still to be cleared up."

By eight o'clock the following morning Nancy was ready to leave the house. She had all the letters for Edgar Nixon in a large envelope of her father's and went with them directly to the postal inspector, Mr. Wernick, who was already at work. He was delighted to hear that most of the mail taken from Ira Nixon had been returned.

"But we have no lead to the guilty person," he told her. "Even that shoe your little friend Tommy gave you must belong to someone else. Shoe prints of Edgar Nixon at Ira's house don't match."

"Too bad," said Nancy.

She told about the letters coming to Edgar Nixon and her suspicions regarding them. When she showed Mr. Wernick the two she had read, he stared in amazement.

"This is very serious," the postal inspector said. "I'll run the rest through our X-ray machine and see if there's money in them."

CHAPTER XIII

Locked In

"How long will it take to X-ray the letters?" Nancy asked the postal inspector.

Mr. Wernick smiled at her. "You're thinking you won't have time to wait? You'd better. I have a hunch there are going to be some surprises in those letters and I'm sure you'll want to know what they are. It won't take long."

He summoned one of the technicians on duty and gave him the assignment. "We suspect there's money inside each of these," he said.

The man was gone only a few minutes. He came back with the X rays as well as the letters. "I'd say there are bills in every envelope. Probably twenty-five dollars in each," he reported.

Nancy was elated and waited for the postal inspector to comment. He said, "I think your idea of a Lonely Hearts Club and money coming in installments is a good one. We'll work on the case from this new angle. And, of course," he added with a twinkle in his eye, "we'll expect all the help we can get from you."

Nancy promised it and said she hoped that before the weekend was over she might have startling news for him. She did not divulge what it was and soon said good-by.

"Oh, the evidence is closing in on Edgar Nixon," she thought. "Now if I can only keep Nancy Smith Drew from marrying him, everything will be wonderful."

She picked up Bess and George, and as they rode toward Emerson, she told about the information she had received at the post office.

The cousins were excited to hear this, but presently Bess said, "Between now and the time that you see Nancy Smith Drew at the play, let's talk about something besides the mysteries. I'd hate to meet Dave with my mind full of clues and crooks."

George could not resist a gibe at her cousin. "That's better than nothing."

Bess made a face and changed the subject. "There's a quaint-looking tearoom ahead. Let's stop there for lunch. It's been a long time since breakfast."

The others agreed, but Nancy said they must not spend too much time. They ate quickly and two hours later the towers of Emerson College came into view. Nancy drove directly to the

Omega Chi Epsilon House, where the girls' dates were on hand to give them a warm welcome.

Ned was tall, handsome, and athletic-looking, with wavy dark hair, a ready smile, and brown eyes.

"I'm glad you made good time," he said, "because I want you to tell us all about this mystery business."

Dave Evans was blond, green-eyed, and of rangy build. He gazed at Bess fondly. "You look stunning in that new suit," he remarked. "I like that fur collar. What is it—squirrel?"

George spoke up. "Yep. She shot it on the way up here."

Bess withered her cousin with a look. "As a matter of fact it's mink."

"How's the play coming?" Nancy asked Burt Eddleton, a short, blond, husky young man.

He shook his head sadly. "Miss Drew hasn't returned yet. I don't know any more about coaching a Shakespearean play than I do about guiding a rocket to the moon. The whole thing's going to be a complete flop."

Nancy was sorry to hear that the actress had not returned yet. She said she had hoped to see Miss Drew for a short time before the afternoon was over.

A short time later Burt announced that he and Dave would have to leave for a rehearsal.

"See you after the show," Dave called as the two boys hurried off.

That evening Ned escorted Nancy, Bess, and George to the college theater, which was attached to the large gymnasium. After the audience was seated, one of the students in the drama group stepped in front of the curtain and said he wished to make an announcement.

"I know all of you are expecting to see a performance of a Shakespearean play. As you have read, the club engaged the services of Miss Smith Drew, a drama coach. Unfortunately she had a sudden errand out of town and has not returned."

Nancy's heart sank. The heiress must have married Edgar Nixon!

The announcer went on, "Late this afternoon, we fellows decided that it would be impossible to put on the play we had planned, so we have substituted a comedy. It is called the *The Mix-up*. We have been rehearsing this for some time, planning to present it in the spring. You won't find it so polished as we had hoped, but we trust you'll enjoy it."

The good-natured audience clapped enthusiastically. The announcer stepped into the wings and the curtain opened. The play was well named and the audience laughed uproariously. The star of the show proved to be Dave. He was so extremely funny, alternately playing a girl and her

twin brother, that the audience broke into repeated applause.

The Mix-up was such a success that Nancy
temporarily forgot her mysteries. But she was
soon to be reminded of them. As she was walking
out of the auditorium, one of Ned's friends spotted her. He called out gaily, "Hi, Nancy Drew!"

At once an attractive young woman, walking
just ahead of Nancy, turned around and stopped.
She smiled at the girl.

"You're Nancy Drew?"

When Nancy nodded, she went on, "For a
moment I thought you might be another Nancy
Drew whom I know. As a matter of fact, I thought
I saw her here tonight but she left before I could
speak to her."

Nancy was excited about this news. "What is
this other Nancy Drew's full name?"

"Nancy Smith Drew."

"Did she ever work for your family?" Nancy
queried.

"Yes, she did. She was a governess for my
brother and me for a few years. She left to become
an actress."

Nancy looked at the young woman. "Are you,
by any chance, Miss Wilson?"

"Yes, I am."

Nancy explained how she had telephoned to
the Wilson home and left a message that if her
mother ever heard from Nancy Smith Drew, she

was to tell her that an inheritance awaited her in England.

"Oh, how marvelous!" Miss Wilson exclaimed. "I've been away at school and my parents didn't pass along the message."

"You said you thought Miss Drew was here tonight?" Nancy asked.

"Yes. I'm sure I saw her in the back of the auditorium when I happened to turn around, just before the show started. I left my seat and tried to find her but couldn't. She went out of the building."

People in the theater had started to crowd past the two girls and now a young man who had been with Miss Wilson came back. After introducing him to Nancy, she told him what they had been talking about.

Nancy said, "Possibly this Nancy Smith Drew is still around. She must have come back for some reason—possibly to see the play. Miss Wilson, could you take a few minutes to help me find her, since you know Miss Drew?"

"I'll be glad to." Miss Wilson turned to the young man, Frank Doolittle, whom Nancy had recognized as one of the star players on the Emerson football squad.

Nancy now introduced Ned, then told him, "We'll be right back. Meet you in front of the theater."

She and Miss Wilson dashed ahead of the others. Reaching the outside, Miss Wilson suddenly exclaimed, "There goes Miss Drew now!" She pointed to a side door of the gymnasium.

The two girls ran like mad, opened the door, and dashed inside. Only a dim light was burning and they could not see very far ahead but realized that the corridor turned abruptly.

"Miss Drew! Miss Drew!" Miss Wilson called. When no response came, Nancy tried her luck, but received no answer.

She and Miss Wilson dashed to the end of the corridor, then turned the corner. They saw no one.

"Wherever could she have been going?" Miss Wilson asked.

Nancy could only guess. "Maybe Miss Drew left some clothes in a locker in one of the rooms. And she wanted to get them, now that she apparently has severed her connection with the Dramatic Club."

The two girls went through another door and this time found themselves at the foot of a flight of metal steps that spiraled both upward and downward. A single unshaded electric bulb illuminated the stairwell feebly.

"Up or down?" Marian Wilson asked.

"Let's go down first," Nancy answered. "Or, let's save time. I'll go down and you go up."

When Nancy reached the floor below she found herself in the furnace room. Sure there would be no lockers here, she turned and scurried up the steps. Miss Wilson was just coming down.

"Nothing up there but a big, dark room and the stairs continue to the roof."

"Miss Drew must have used another exit," Nancy speculated. "Well, I guess all we can do is leave."

At that moment the light went out.

"Oh dear!" her companion cried. "They're turning out the lights and locking up!"

The two girls dashed along the corridor, feeling the walls until they came to the outer door. Nancy tried to lift the long bar which opened it, but this would not budge.

"We're locked in!" she exclaimed, and began banging on the door with her fist and crying, "Let us out! We're trapped!"

There was not a sound from outside.

"Whatever will we do?" Marian Wilson asked nervously.

"Frankly I don't know, but let me think a minute." A few moments later Nancy said, "That dark room you saw—were there any windows in it?"

"Yes, several."

"Maybe we can get out that way," Nancy suggested.

The girls groped their way along the corridor and up the spiral stairway. They opened the door

to the dark room and made their way toward one
of the windows. To their dismay, chicken wire
was tacked over it and the window could not be
opened. All the others had been protected the
same way.

"I wonder which side of the theater this is on,"
Nancy speculated. "If we could only attract someone's attention!"

"But how?" Marian Wilson asked.

"I guess we'll have to break the glass and yell."

"But the chicken wire was put up there so the
glass wouldn't get broken," Marian pointed out.

Nancy said she realized this, but hoped that a
hard blow would break the wire as well as the
glass. She began to feel around the floor with her
feet, hoping to locate some heavy object. Presently
she found what felt like a cannon ball. She assumed it was a ball used for shot-put contests.

There was enough light outside for the girls to
see anyone going by. As Nancy picked up the metal ball, Marian Wilson exclaimed, "I just saw a
car drive up! Nancy Smith Drew got into it!"

Nancy rushed forward, hoping to break the
glass and attract the young woman's attention.
But in a second the car was gone. A feeling of
exasperation came over her. Suppose no one else
came past whose attention she could attract!

"Here come a couple of boys. Quick! Break
the glass!" Marian cried out.

Nancy heaved the heavy ball and it did the

"Let us out! We're trapped!" Nancy cried

trick. The chicken wire bent and the glass shattered.

"They heard it!" Marian cried out, jumping up and down hopefully.

Together, the two girls screamed out, "Ned! Frank!"

The boys looked around.

"Up here!" Nancy called. "We're locked in upstairs in the gym!"

Ned and Frank gazed upward in astonishment. "How'd you get there?" Frank asked.

"It's a long story," Marian replied. "Spooky in here. I don't like it."

"We'll have you out in a minute," Ned said.

The two boys raced off to find the grounds superintendent so he could open the door. Meanwhile, the girls groped their way down the stairs and were waiting at the door when it was finally opened.

"Thanks," they said, locking arms with their dates.

"Boy! What were you trying to do?" Frank asked.

"Catch up with an actress," said Nancy, chuckling. "You missed a chance for some excitement."

An explanation was quickly given. Nancy ended the story with the rueful statement that Nancy Smith Drew had disappeared again.

"What! Then coach was *here*. That's a funny one," Frank remarked.

Ned said, "Pretty shabby way to treat the Emerson Drama Club."

Nancy suddenly had an idea. "Ned," she said, "let's get my car and go to the place where Nancy Smith Drew lives. Maybe we can still stop her from getting married to Edgar Nixon!"

The two said good-by to the other couple and dashed off toward the fraternity house. They had almost reached it when a large rock came whizzing through the air. It was aimed directly at Nancy!

CHAPTER XIV

Elusive Niece

NED had caught a glimpse of the rock coming in Nancy's direction. Instantly he pulled her down to the pavement and the stone sailed over the girl's head. It crashed through one of the fraternity-house windows.

"Oh!" Nancy exclaimed, looking around quickly to see the person who had thrown the rock.

Both she and Ned saw a man running toward the parking lot. They dashed after him. Ned soon outdistanced Nancy and in a final sprint overtook the fellow, who was rather shabbily dressed.

Ned grabbed hold of the assailant's collar and yanked him around. "What was the big idea?" he said angrily. "You might have harmed my friend badly."

"But I didn't, so let me go!" the stranger retorted.

"I'll do nothing of the kind," Ned snapped. "Suppose you give me an explanation. Then I'll decide what to do."

By this time Nancy had joined them. She, too, demanded to know why the man had acted the way he had and what his name was.

Their captive began to tremble with fright. "I—I really didn't mean no harm, miss," he said. "Please don't make me tell my name. It'll be bad for me."

"Why?" Nancy said. "Would you rather tell the police?"

"Oh no! Not the police!" the man pleaded. "As I said, I didn't hurt you when I threw the stone, so you got no right to hold me. Let me go!"

Nancy and Ned looked at each other. Legally the man was right. He could insist that he had not intended to hit Nancy or the window with the stone.

"You should pay for repairing the window," Nancy said.

"I ain't got no money."

"In that case, I guess the police will have to decide what to do," Ned told him.

"Please, mister, don't do that. I'll tell you my name. It's Otto Busch. I'm just a no-good guy in this town. I'll tell you the whole story. A smooth-lookin' guy came up to me down in the village and asked me if I'd like to earn some money."

"Yes?" Nancy prodded the man as he paused.

"Well, he gave me a few dollars to do a job. He showed me a picture of you, miss, and said when you come home tonight, here at this house, I was to throw a big-sized rock at you and scare you."

"Scare me about what?" Nancy queried, staring hard at Otto Busch.

The man shrugged. "I dunno. The guy didn't say. I s'posed he had something on you." Busch stopped speaking.

"Is that all?" Ned asked.

"Yeah. Now can I go?"

Nancy asked for a description of the man and was sure he was Edgar Nixon. He must be getting desperate to try such a villainous method to keep her from trying to solve the mystery about him. Perhaps he had found out she had taken the letters for his Lonely Hearts Club to the postal inspector in River Heights.

Ned let go his hold on Otto Busch. "I advise you not to be doing errands for people you don't know. How much did the man pay you for this job?"

"Twenty-five dollars."

"That's pretty high pay for throwing one stone," Ned remarked. "Suppose you turn over some of it to me to have a new window put in our fraternity house."

Otto was reluctant to do this, but seeing the determined look in the husky football player's eyes, he changed his mind and handed over five dollars. Then, quick as a ferret, he dashed off among the cars.

"We may as well let him go," said Nancy.

"What a night!" Ned remarked. "Nancy, you must be dead tired. Why don't you go to bed and let me pick you up early in the morning to go to the house where Miss Nancy Smith Drew has been living?"

When Nancy demurred, he added, "I'll tell you what I'll do. I'll drive past the place myself. If there's a light in the house, I'll ring the bell. If the elusive heiress is home, I'll have her telephone you."

"I guess," Nancy mused, "that the man who left the money to his niece had no idea she would be so hard to find."

Nancy suddenly realized she was extremely weary and consented to the arrangement. She waited up for half an hour but no phone call came and finally she went to bed.

True to his word, Ned was ready by eight-thirty the next morning to take her to Mrs. Roderick's guesthouse on Linden Road. The owner was a pleasant, middle-aged woman and her house looked immaculate.

"Miss Drew?" she said when asked about her guest. "She slept here last night, but she has already gone out." The woman smiled. "She is busy buying a trousseau."

Nancy asked quickly, "Is she wearing a wedding ring?"

Mrs. Roderick laughed. "No, but after that little trip she just made, Miss Drew returned with a beautiful engagement ring."

"When will she be back?" Nancy inquired, trying not to show her mounting excitement.

"She didn't say. Miss Drew was carrying a suitcase, and I expect she planned to do a lot of shopping and fill it up."

Nancy and Ned exchanged glances. Was it possible the actress would not return?

At once Mrs. Roderick asked, "Is something the matter?"

"I don't know," Nancy replied. "I have been trying hard to find Miss Drew because I have a very important message for her. I can't reveal everything, but when your Miss Drew returns, tell her another Nancy Drew was here and must speak to her at once. Above all, she *mustn't* get married until I talk with her."

Mrs. Roderick started in surprise. "You mean there is something the matter with the man she's going to marry?"

Nancy said she preferred not to say anything more. "But, Mrs. Roderick, please be sure to have Miss Drew get in touch with me at the Omega Chi Epsilon House."

The woman stared in bafflement. "I assure you Miss Drew is a lovely person. Surely she would not be doing something underhanded."

"Oh, I'm not accusing her of doing anything underhanded," Nancy replied. "But she may be doing something too hastily."

She and Ned decided to leave before Mrs. Roderick could think of any further questions. Nancy thanked her, asked the woman to give Miss Drew the message, and hurried back to the convertible.

As they drove into the campus, Ned headed the car for the gymnasium. "I'm due to report," he said. "I'll see you after the game."

Nancy patted his arm and wished him all kinds of good luck. "I'll be rooting for you at the top of my lungs," she added as he grinned and got out of the car.

She slid over to the driver's seat and turned in the direction of the fraternity house. Suddenly Nancy had a hunch and took a road that led to the Town Hall. She rushed inside and up to the Marriage License Bureau. The clerk on duty smiled when she eagerly asked if a Nancy Smith Drew had obtained a license recently.

"No. Guess you'll have to try some other town around here if you want to find her. Is she a friend of yours?"

"Sort of," Nancy replied. "Anyway I must find Miss Drew. If, by any chance, she should come here, tell her another Nancy Drew at the Omega Chi Epsilon House simply *must* see her before she gets married."

The clerk blinked. "Sounds like a mystery thriller." he remarked.

Nancy did not comment. After thanking him, she dashed from the building and hurried to her car.

On her way once more, Nancy mulled over the case. "I have a strong hunch Miss Drew isn't going back to Mrs. Roderick's—at least not for a while. Suppose—just suppose Edgar Nixon has thought out a whole new scheme to escape being caught. Now what could it be?"

Nancy discarded many theories, then one popped into her mind that she felt was worth pursuing. "It's just possible Edgar plans to take his bride to London. Then, as if quite by accident, she'll learn of her inheritance. He'll see to it that she doesn't find out in the United States."

She parked the car and entered the fraternity house. Nearly everyone was out, and no one was using the telephone.

"I think I'll call up the overseas airlines leaving from New York."

She got the list of numbers from information and then began calling. Between long waits, due either to busy lines, or the reservation clerks having to look up the information, half an hour went with no luck.

"Well, here goes for the last one." Nancy sighed as she dialed the number.

In a few minutes a pleasant voice answered. Nancy put the same question. "Have you a reservation for today or someday soon for a Mr. and Mrs. Edgar Nixon, or Mr. Nixon and Miss Nancy Smith Drew?"

"Just a minute."

The reservations girl came back on the wire. "Hello? . . . Yes, they leave on—"

The connection was suddenly cut off.

CHAPTER XV

A Worse Mix-up

THOUGH Nancy tried over and over again to call
the airline back, the wire continued to be busy.

"Oh phooey!" she said to herself impatiently.

Suddenly Nancy realized that she still did not
know if the reservation was for Mr. and Mrs.
Edgar Nixon, or for Edgar and Nancy Smith
Drew. Also, she had not found out whether or not
they were going to London, nor on what day they
were flying.

Before trying the airline again, Nancy had to
relinquish the phone to several students who
wanted to make calls. Soon the fraternity house
held a mob of chattering, laughing boys and girls.
Even if Nancy could have made the connection,
she would not have heard what was being said
at the other end of the line.

Bess and George came running up to her.
"Nancy, we've been looking all over for you. It's

almost lunchtime," said Bess. "My, you look as if you're in the doldrums instead of having fun. What's the matter?"

Nancy brought her friends up to date on the latest clue. "Well, here goes one more try for the airline."

The cousins could tell by the expression on Nancy's face that the line was still busy. Finally George said, "If Miss Drew didn't tell Mrs. Roderick she was going away, she's probably coming back so you can talk to her later. Come on. Time to eat, and then we'll have to hurry off to the game."

Nancy was torn between two desires. She hated to give up her pursuit of the other Nancy Drew. On the other hand, she would not miss seeing Ned play in this big and final game of the football season for anything.

At that instant the telephone rang and Nancy answered it. "Chi Omega Epsilon House?" a young woman's voice asked.

"Yes."

"I'd like to speak to Nancy Drew."

"You're talking to her. Is this Marian Wilson?"

"Yes. Nancy, I'm so glad I got you before you left."

"Any news about Miss Drew?" Nancy asked her.

"No, I haven't seen her. I drove around town, thinking I might get a glimpse of her, but she wasn't in sight."

Marian Wilson said she had a request to make. "Since both Ned and Frank are playing, how about you and I attending the game together?"

"I think that's a wonderful idea," said Nancy. "You know, there's just an outside chance that Nancy Smith Drew may be there, and you can spot her."

It was arranged that Marian was to come over to the fraternity house directly after lunch and go to the game with the girls. Dave and Burt, who were on the second-string team, had left already for the stadium.

An hour later, just as Nancy was about to leave the house with the group, a telephone call came from her father. "You must have something important to tell me," she said quickly.

"I have tracked down the firm which offered to present Nancy Smith Drew so she can claim her inheritance."

"What kind of an agency is it?" his daughter inquired.

"A shady outfit and not to be trusted."

Nancy was excited at the news. "Maybe the agency's story is a fake, and some impostor is going to appear calling herself Nancy Smith Drew."

"That's what Mr. Bates-Jones thinks," her father said.

She told him all that she had learned the night before and during the morning. "Your clue gives me an idea, Dad. Maybe Edgar Nixon doesn't intend to marry Nancy Smith Drew at all. Instead, he's taking her away to keep her from being found by me."

"It's a good guess," the lawyer remarked.

"And here's another thing," Nancy went on. "Perhaps Edgar Nixon is already married to somebody else who is in cahoots with him and is going to play the part."

Mr. Drew sighed. "This mystery gets to be more mixed up all the time. Well, Nancy, I advise you to forget the whole thing for the afternoon and evening. Enjoy the game and have fun at the dance tonight."

Nancy laughed. "I don't promise to forget the mystery, but I know I'll have a marvelous time. Good-by, Dad. Take care."

On the way to the game, Nancy brought her friends up to date on the latest development.

Marian Wilson was shocked. "We mustn't let that lovely Miss Drew be swindled!" she cried.

Bess spoke up. "Nancy is doing everything she can. She has left messages everywhere for Nancy Smith Drew not to get married and to get in touch with her immediately. Now let's concentrate on the game." The girls agreed and Nancy said no more about the mystery.

There was a huge crowd on hand for this important game between Emerson and State University. Vendors stood outside the stadium selling pennants and football pins, and hats and flowers of the colors of the two colleges. Inside, the bands of both schools were playing. This, together with whistles and high-pitched conversation, made a great din. It turned to thunderous applause and cheers as the two teams trotted onto the field.

Nancy and her friends had seats ideally located near the center of the field. They cheered lustily, then quieted as a whistle was blown by the referee and the captains of the opposing teams met to confer with the officials.

"Emerson receives the kick!" came the announcement over the loudspeaker.

The ball sailed through the air. The game was on! The blue jerseys of State U swept down the field.

"Frank's catching it!" Marian cried out as the ball came down.

After deftly side-stepping a would-be tackler, Frank cut to his left, and with a good block from Ned Nickerson, sped to the thirty-yard line before being tackled.

Excitement ran high in the stands, packed solid with spectators in red, blue, and green sports clothes. Pennants waved amid the laughter and cheering spectators.

"Now watch Ned go!" Nancy said. "Come on, Ned, touchdown!"

On the playing field, Ned Nickerson realized

there was no magic formula for conquering State
U. He passed to a halfback, who tried an end
sweep. It was good for three yards.

On the next play Ned faded back to pass, but
apparently State U had scouted him well, because two linebackers came charging through. His
toss was rushed and fell short of the receiver. A
groan went up from Emerson.

Ned himself tried an off-tackle slant but failed
to make the necessary ten yards. Then he dropped back to punt. The ball soared high and far,
giving Emerson defenders plenty of time to race
down the field. The State receiver was stopped
in his tracks as Emerson fans roared their approval.

"Come on, State! Sock it to 'em!" came cries
from across the field, but State fared no better.
They also had to kick on fourth down. Frank
again received the ball. But instead of running
with it, he lateraled to Ned. The speedy quarterback dived, ducked, wriggled, and side-stepped as
he flew up the field.

"Stop him! Stop him!" screamed State's rooters.

Now there was only one man between Ned and
the goal line. The quarterback tried to side-step
him.

Slam! With a bone-jarring tackle, Ned was
brought to the turf twelve feet short of a six-
pointer. He rose slowly from the ground and
limped back into the huddle, but his chest hurt.

"You all right?" Frank asked him.

"Sure. Just shaken up a little. Let's give 'em the down-and-out pass pattern."

When the ball was snapped, Ned rolled back and to his left. Emerson's left end faked out the opposing halfback and dashed toward the corner of the field. Ned rifled a pass. It was a perfect pitch. The end caught it in his upstretched arms and fell across the goal line!

"Eeh! Yeeh!" Marian exclaimed, jumping up and down and waving her arms wildly.

Emerson stands were a bedlam of noise and motion. Their team led, 6–0.

"Come on, Ned!" Nancy cried out. "Make it seven!"

She felt confident about Ned's place-kicking. The sportswriters had praised his toe. Now he would add to their score!

As Ned walked back into the huddle, he was still wincing with the pain in his chest. The teams faced each other. State's linemen were poised, ready to spring forward at the snap of the ball.

The ball was passed low to Frank. He set it up for the kick. Ned's leg came forward, his toe hit the ball, and sent it sailing into the air as the spectators rose to their feet. There was dead silence for an instant, then a deafening roar.

No good! The referee's motion indicated that the ball had missed by inches.

"That's a shame," Marian said.

"What happened to the great Nickerson?" a State fan yelled. "He better go to another college where he can learn how to punt."

Nancy was concentrating on Ned. "Oh dear, I hope nothing has happened to him," she said to Marian. "He was limping a little."

Suddenly Nancy's hand flew to her mouth as she stifled a shriek. "Oh no!"

Ned Nickerson had collapsed on the green turf.

CHAPTER XVI

Mistaken Identity

INSTANTLY Frank called for time out. The water boy rushed onto the field, followed by the Emerson trainer. Nancy rose from her seat, excused herself as she stepped in front of other spectators, and finally made it to the aisle.

Worried, Nancy hastened down the concrete steps toward the field. By the time she reached the railing, Ned was being carried from the field by Frank and the trainer.

"Ned! Ned!" she cried out, but he did not hear her as the trainer eased him carefully onto the bench. Players crowded around quickly and Nancy lost sight of her friend.

Marian came to stand at Nancy's side. "I'm sure he'll be all right, honey," she said consolingly. "Ned has been hurt before and always managed to return to the game."

Suddenly Nancy saw Frank walking away from

the bench toward the field, where the men were waiting to resume play.

"Frank, is he all right?" Nancy cried out. The fullback turned and waved at the two girls, but said nothing.

"Come on. Let's get back to our seats," Marian said.

Nancy only half-watched the game. Her mind was on Ned. But nothing spectacular happened. It was a defensive battle with each side gaining a few yards, then being forced to kick to its opponent.

During the half-time period, the marching band performed, but the colorful formations were lost on Nancy because she was worried about Ned. But when the players trotted back, she relaxed. Ned was among them!

"Oh!" she said with a sigh of relief. Ned, however, remained benched. Emerson's defenses could well have used him the two periods that followed. State's backfield gained momentum. Finally they were on the two-yard line of Emerson.

"Hold that line! Hold that line!" Nancy screamed along with the Emerson rooting section.

But on the next play State scored. Now the cry arose, "Block that kick! Block that kick!"

The teams lined up. Toe met ball. Good! The score stood 7–6 in favor of State U.

Nancy and Marian screamed themselves hoarse

as the autumn shadows settled over the stadium and a brisk wind began to blow across the field.

"Oh dear," Nancy said. "Only three minutes left, Marian."

The score was still 7–6. The Emerson substitute quarterback was doing a good job, but lacked Ned's field generalship. The boys tried, but it was obvious to all that they were tiring. At last Emerson worked the ball down to State's thirty-five-yard line. It was fourth down.

"They'll have to kick," Marian said.

"Wait! Look!" Nancy cried.

On the sideline Ned was trotting back and forth. After a quick word from the coach, he snatched his helmet and put it on as he ran onto the field.

"A kick!" the spectators yelled. "Nickerson's going to kick!"

As the two sides lined up, every spectator in the stadium rose to his feet, cheering. The distance to the goal post seemed impossible!

Ned braced himself. The ball was snapped. Frank placed it down.

Thud! The ball arched high and sped through the air. Would it make the crossbar? Would the wind blow it to one side?

The answer came in a deafening roar from the Emerson side. Ned had scored! Three more points went up on the scoreboard—Emerson 9, State U 7. Colored streamers flew down from the stands, and confetti rained over the delirious spectators.

"Ned did it!" Nancy screamed. "He won the game!"

Minutes later it was all over. Emerson fans flooded onto the field. They hoisted Ned to their shoulders and carried him to the dresssing room.

Nancy was waiting by the door as Ned stepped out later. "You were simply magnificent," she said.

The next second Nancy's expression changed completely. Ned noticed it at once. "What's the matter?"

"Oh, I don't want to take away any of the glory from the celebration," she said, "but I just saw a man over there who looks like Edgar Nixon!"

Burt and Dave, who had come out with Ned, offered to dash across to where the man was and detain him until Nancy could get there.

"Ned, please wait here," Nancy requested, and sprinted after the two boys.

But by the time she reached them, the man they had stopped was laughing. Nancy heard him say, "No, I'm not Edgar Nixon."

Burt turned to introduce Nancy. "This is the young lady who thought you were someone she's looking for."

"I'm terribly sorry," she said. "From a distance you looked like a man named Edgar Nixon."

The man continued to grin. "You know twice today I've been mistaken for that person. And both times by very pretty young ladies."

Nancy blushed as she asked who the other young lady was.

The stranger replied, "I don't know her name but she said she was an actress."

Nancy was puzzled. If the person was Nancy Smith Drew and had met Edgar Nixon at the guesthouse in Ridgefield, surely she would know what he looked like.

The man she had detained was saying, "I'd like to meet this double of mine someday."

"When did you talk to this actress?" Nancy asked.

"Just before the game. She said her date was supposed to meet her for lunch at the hotel. I'm staying there."

"Is Mr. Nixon there too?" Dave spoke up.

"I don't know."

When Ned heard the story, he insisted upon accompanying Nancy downtown and inquiring at the hotel for Edgar Nixon and Nancy Smith Drew. To her disappointment, she found that neither was registered.

"If Edgar Nixon is in town, he'll probably be at one of the guesthouses or motels," Ned suggested.

"Ned," Nancy said quietly, "you were hurt in the game today. Don't you think you ought to go back to your room and rest?"

The football player shook his head. "I'm all

right now. The wind was knocked out of me and I got dizzy and faint for a while. No, I insist upon going with you on this hunt."

Nancy beamed at him. "You're certainly a good sport."

Ned laughed. "I don't want to lose my girl to some kook. If you do come across Edgar Nixon while you're alone, he may harm you."

Nancy and Ned's errand proved to be futile. Neither the suspect nor Nancy Smith Drew was known at any of the places where they asked. To be sure that he was not using an alias Nancy showed the picture she had borrowed from Ira. In each case the person she consulted insisted that no one who looked like him had stayed there recently and most of them did not recall ever having seen him.

On their way back to the campus, Nancy said, "Ned, let's stop at Mrs. Roderick's. She may have some word about Miss Drew."

Nancy fervently hoped that the actress might even be there. Again she was disappointed. Mrs. Roderick said that Miss Drew had not returned.

"She must have filled her suitcase with new clothes and left Emerson. After what you told me, I just haven't been able to stop worrying about Miss Drew."

Nancy mentioned the possibility that the actress and the man she planned to marry had left

Emerson to go to London. "May I call the airline and find out more about it? I was cut off when talking to them this morning."

"Certainly," Mrs. Roderick said. "I only have one phone. It's in the kitchen. Help yourself."

This time Nancy was able to put through a satisfactory call. She learned that a Mr. Edgar Nixon had a reservation on the nine-thirty Monday night plane to London. His wife had canceled.

"Thank you very much," she said. "Now will you please look and see if you have a reservation for a Miss Nancy Smith Drew?"

After a few minutes she was told that the airline did have a reservation for a person by that name. Nancy hung up and walked back to the living room where Mrs. Roderick and Ned were waiting. She reported what she had learned.

"The question now is whether this is the Edgar Nixon I'm looking for. And is Nancy Smith Drew the real one or a person who is going to present herself as the heiress?"

Mrs. Roderick shook her head. "What a dreadful mess this is! Well, I hope you are able to settle it."

"I'm afraid," said Nancy, "that Edgar Nixon intends to marry the Nancy Smith Drew who will inherit the money, but I'm hoping I can prevent the marriage."

"How in the world can you do that?" the woman asked.

Ned spoke up with a smile. "I can guess," he said. "It wouldn't surprise me if Nancy intends to take off for New York and stop the couple from flying to London."

Nancy giggled. "How well you know me! That's exactly what I have in mind."

"Well, I wish you luck," Mrs. Roderick said. "And when you have a chance, do drop me a postcard and tell me how everything comes out."

"I'll do that," Nancy promised. She thanked the woman for being so cooperative.

It was dark when Nancy and Ned came out of the house. They were pleased it was a clear crisp evening for the dance.

When they reached the fraternity parking lot, it was full. "We'll have to leave your car in the street," Ned remarked.

Nancy, who was at the wheel, turned around and headed down the street. Parking was allowed only on one side and she had to go to the next block before finding a space.

Ned teased her by saying he was sure she would never squeeze her convertible in such a tight parking place. However, after several skillful twists of the wheel, Nancy maneuvered the car in the vacant spot. Ned admitted he could not have done a finer job.

Nancy locked up the convertible. Then she and Ned started walking on the side of the street where no cars were allowed to be parked.

About halfway back to the fraternity house, they suddenly became aware of bright lights behind them. The two turned automatically. To their horror, a car had raced up over the curb and was heading directly at them!

CHAPTER XVII

Fake Summons

THOUGH terrified, Nancy and Ned reacted quickly. With a tremendous leap they managed to get out of the way of the oncoming car. The couple landed on some tree roots and lost their balance.

Suddenly it was dark around them. They realized that the driver of the car which had almost hit them had turned off his headlights. In a second the car roared back into the street and sped away.

Nancy and Ned picked themselves up and stared after the vehicle. By a street light they caught a glimpse of the car. It was red in color.

The driver deliberately tried to run us down," Ned stormed. "That was your enemy, Nancy."

"I'm afraid so," she agreed. "Ned, we must report this to the police at once. Let's go back to my car and drive downtown."

"Are you sure you're all right?" Ned asked solicitously. "You don't want to go back to the fraternity house first?"

Nancy assured him her nerves were steady now. "I'm just mad," she said. "The person in that car was either Edgar Nixon or one of his henchmen. I'm going to keep after him until he's brought to justice!"

Ned laughed. "That a girl!" he said, patting her shoulder.

At police headquarters they talked to Captain Krate. Ned told of the recent near-accident, then Nancy went on to reveal her suspicions about a man named Edgar Nixon who ran a Lonely Hearts Club.

"Lonely Hearts Club, eh?" the captain repeated. He turned the pages of a large book on his desk. "I have a notation here to be on the lookout for such a person. We've had complaints from two women who said that an Edgar Nixon promised them a husband. But he never produced any."

"How did the club operate?" Nancy asked.

Captain Krate said that the total sum for finding a husband was one hundred dollars which was paid on the installment plan of twenty-five dollars a month.

"These poor women sent their last payment but never heard from Nixon again. When they made inquiries at the houses where he had lived, they learned that he had moved away and left no forwarding address.

Nancy reported how she had come upon one such address and seen a couple of letters, each one containing twenty-five dollars. "But by that time he had moved."

"That's always the pattern," Captain Krate remarked. "Do you know the names of any of his victims?"

"Possibly one," she replied. "Her name is the same as mine. That's how I became mixed up in the mystery."

Nancy told him about the actress by the name of Nancy Smith Drew. "I'm so afraid she's not only a victim of Edgar Nixon's dishonesty, but that he intends to marry her and help himself to an inheritance she's going to get."

The police captain frowned. "This is a complicated case. Well, I shall put out an alarm also for this Miss Nancy Smith Drew."

Nancy then left with Ned and went back to the fraternity house. Bess and George were already in the girls' bedroom and were amazed at the story she had to tell about the near-accident.

"It seems as if you aren't safe anywhere," Bess said. "Nancy, please be careful."

"I promise," Nancy said with a chuckle. "But my enemy seems to strike in such peculiar ways, all I can do is jump out of his path as fast as possible."

She hurried to take a shower and get dressed for the dance. Dinner was merry and afterward the couples strolled off to the gymnasium where the dance was to be held.

Football star Ned Nickerson became the center of attention with congratulations, handshaking, and backslapping the order of the evening. Finally, as the band began to play, he escaped onto the dance floor with Nancy.

The evening was about half over and Nancy and Ned were seated on one side of the gym when a boy came up and said that Ned was wanted on the telephone. He excused himself to Nancy and hurried off.

A moment later the band started a lively tune and one by one couples began to go back onto the dance floor. Bess, George, Burt, and Dave waved to Nancy as they passed by. At that moment the music suddenly stopped and the drums began to roll. Everyone became quiet and listened attentively.

The band leader called out, "Where is Nancy Drew?"

"Here I am!" Nancy said, jumping up and raising her hand.

"Will you please step up here," the leader requested. "The police want to see you."

As Nancy hurried forward, a gasp went up around the room. Why did the police want to see her?

When she reached the band, the young leader said, "I'm sorry I had to call out that way, but I didn't know you. Hope you don't mind."

"Not at all," said Nancy. "Tell me, what's this about the police?"

She was told that two detectives were waiting for her on the stage of the adjoining theater. "The student who came to give us the message said that they have news for you of the other Miss Drew."

Excitedly Nancy hurried from the gymnasium and down the long corridor which led to the stage in the theater. The entrance door was open and footlights were on. The curtain had been hoisted about halfway up.

Nancy looked around but did not see anyone. Where were the detectives?

"Hello!" she called out, thinking they might have walked out into the far wings, where the dressing rooms were.

There was no answer. Nancy was puzzled and turned to look out over the darkened seats. As she stood pondering directly under the curtain, she heard a noise above her. A sixth sense told the young detective to move in a hurry. She jumped forward just as the heavy curtain crashed to the floor.

Terror seized Nancy. She leaped across the footlights to the floor and sped as if on wings to the corridor leading to the gym. She had not gone far when she was met by Ned. Bess, George, Burt, and Dave were following.

"What's up?" Ned asked, seeing the look of fright on Nancy's face.

Turning, Nancy pointed back toward the stage. "In there! The message was a hoax! Someone tried to kill me by dropping the curtain!"

Bess shrieked and held onto Nancy. "Don't go back in there!"

"She's right," said Burt. "You girls stay here. We'll find out what's going on in the theater."

Nancy, still shaken by what had happened, agreed to wait in the corridor with the other girls.

The three boys were gone for several minutes, then returned to report they had found no one. Everyone was upset over the incident.

"Let's find the person who brought the message to the band leader," George suggested.

Ned turned to the other boys. "Isn't Jim Hankin on duty outside the gym tonight?" he asked.

"Yes, I think he is."

Ned explained that Jim was the guard for the evening to turn away from the dance anyone who was not invited.

The group went at once to speak to him. Jim said a plainclothesman had come up to him and showed a badge. The detective said he did not want to intrude and asked that a student take the message to Nancy.

*Nancy jumped forward just as the curtain crashed
to the floor*

"I didn't know her, so I asked our band leader to do it," Jim explained.

He was quickly told what had happened and looked worried. "I don't think that man will show up around here again, but if he does, I'll sure hold onto him and yell for help."

Nancy spoke up. "What did the man look like?"

She rather expected Jim to describe Edgar Nixon, but was told that the fake plainclothesman was tall, heavy-set, and had blond hair. Nancy assumed he was a pal of Edgar Nixon.

The Lonely Hearts Club suspect probably did not want to take a chance on being identified and had sent someone else. He was probably an out-of-towner, not known to the Emerson police.

Nancy and her friends returned to the dance, but they did not wait until it was over. Though Nancy hated to admit it, she was exhausted. The day had been a strenuous one for Ned and he also was pretty tired.

Everyone slept soundly, but was up in time the next morning to go the special chapel service arranged for students and their dates. As soon as it was over, Nancy and Ned returned to the Omega Chi Epsilon House. The telephone was ringing and the call proved to be for Nancy.

"It's from a Mrs. Gruen," she was told by the student on duty at the time.

Nancy picked up the receiver and said, "Hello. Is everything all right?"

"I'm fine and your father is too," the housekeeper said, "but things are not well with Ira Nixon. His brother came last night and robbed him!"

CHAPTER XVIII

Shakespearean Puzzle

HANNAH Gruen explained to Nancy that after church she had taken some food to poor Ira Nixon.

"He was in a bad state," she reported. "The theft occurred late last night. Edgar came there and pounded on the door until Ira let him in. He never so much as asked how Ira was feeling, or when he was going back to work or anything. That dreadful Edgar started right in demanding money."

"You mean part of the inheritance?"

"No, no. Edgar said Ira always had been a miser and he was sure he had money hidden in the house. When Ira wouldn't answer him, Edgar started hunting for some himself."

Nancy was shocked at the story. She asked if Edgar had found any money.

"That's the dreadful part of it," Mrs. Gruen

went on. "Ira did have some in the house—lots of it. He was very foolish not to have put it in a bank."

"How did Edgar get hold of the money?" Nancy queried.

"He stole it," the housekeeper said. "Edgar Nixon practically tore the house apart. He ripped sofa cushions, bed pillows, and emptied every drawer in the house."

"How dreadful!" Nancy exclaimed. "Do you know how much money he got?"

The answer stunned her. "One thousand dollars!"

"Oh no!" Nancy cried out. "Poor Ira! How was he feeling when you left him?"

"Pretty bad," Mrs. Gruen replied. "I warmed up the food I took and made him eat some of it. This quieted him a bit, but I kept telling him he should notify the police. He refuses to and wouldn't let me."

Nancy was incensed. But she could see that Ira, despite his family misfortune, did not want any unfavorable publicity about his half brother. After all, they did have the same mother.

"I thought I'd better call you, Nancy, and tell you right away," Mrs. Gruen said. "What do you think should be done?"

Nancy asked the housekeeper if she had spoken to Mr. Drew about it. "No, I haven't had a chance. After church, your father went out into the country to see a client. He was planning to have dinner there."

For several seconds Nancy sat lost in thought. Finally Mrs. Gruen said, "Nancy, are you still there?"

"Yes. I'm just thinking. Wait until I get back before doing anything. We girls are heading home this afternoon."

She quickly told Hannah Gruen what had happened at Emerson and said that actually she was no closer to finding either Edgar Nixon or Nancy Smith Drew than she had been days ago.

"Well, Hannah dear, I guess I'd better hang up now. Ned and the others are waiting for me to have lunch. I'll see you around suppertime."

At the lunch table Nancy told her friends about the latest twist in the mystery. Her friends were dismayed, and Dave remarked, "Edgar Nixon is one of the slipperiest crooks I've ever heard of."

Nancy said, "Before we girls leave Emerson, I'd like to call on Mrs. Roderick once more. It's just possible she has heard from Nancy Smith Drew but hasn't bothered to telephone me about it."

Bess and George offered to do Nancy's packing while she was gone. In a little while she and Ned rode off in the convertible.

When Mrs. Roderick opened her front door, she exclaimed, "You're just the people I want to see! I was going to call you, Nancy, but I couldn't remember which fraternity house you said you were in."

"You have news of Miss Drew?" Nancy asked.

"Indeed I do. Please come inside and sit down. I'm so weak from the shock I just had that my knees are still wobbly."

They all went into the living room and sat down. Mrs. Roderick explained that she taught a Sunday-school class and then went to church service afterward.

"I thought for a change I'd stay out to dinner, so I went to a tearoom that's open on Sunday. This was the reason I didn't get home until a a little while ago."

So far, there was nothing about Mrs. Roderick's story to upset her. Nancy and Ned waited patiently for her to go on.

"As soon as I came into the house, I went upstairs to change my clothes. To get to my bedroom, I had to pass Miss Drew's door. When I glanced into the room, I saw something on the bureau. This seemed funny to me so I went in to look at it."

Mrs. Roderick went on to say that lying on the bureau was two weeks' room rent but no explanation by Miss Drew as to why she had left it.

"I thought I'd better investigate to see if her clothes and jewelry and everything were gone.

Sure enough they were. There's no question but that she moved out."

Nancy asked Mrs. Roderick if Miss Drew had left any kind of a message.

"Oh yes," the woman said, "but it didn't say anything personal—wasn't even addressed to me. In fact it really wasn't a note. Just a lot of words scribbled on a piece of paper."

Neither Nancy nor Ned was sure this was the case but hesitated to ask to see the note.

"You know how eager we are to find Miss Drew," Nancy said. "If you have no idea where she's going, do you mind if I look around her room for a clue?"

"No, go ahead," Mrs. Roderick said, and led the young people upstairs.

She watched in interest as the couple made a thorough search of the place. Finally they admitted defeat.

Nancy turned to Mrs. Roderick. "Are you sure that Miss Drew came here herself?"

The woman looked startled. Then she answered slowly, "No, I'm not. And nobody else around here would have seen who it was. We're church-going folks on this street, so everyone would have been out."

"Then it's just possible," Nancy said, "that someone else could have used Miss Drew's key and come in."

"I suppose so," Mrs. Roderick agreed. Suddenly she turned and looked straight at the couple. "Are you two detectives?" she asked.

The young people began to laugh, then Ned said, "I'm not, but Nancy Drew is the best girl detective in the whole world!"

"Don't you believe him," Nancy said quickly. "I have solved some mysteries, I'll admit, and I enjoy it, but I'm sure there are many other girls who could do the same."

Mrs. Roderick was silent a few moments, then she said, "I think I'd better show you that paper with the funny notes on it. I put it in my room. See what you can make out of the thing."

She went to get it and soon returned, holding a sheet of white paper on which several verses were written in small handwriting. Nancy and Ned read them quickly.

"These are quotations from Shakespeare," Nancy told Mrs. Roderick.

"Shakespeare? Then I suppose it's not so funny," the woman remarked, "since Miss Drew was coaching the Shakespearean play."

Ned requested that Nancy read the various lines aloud. She did so, pausing between each quotation and puckering her brow. They said:

My mind is troubled, like a fountain stirr'd;
And I myself see not the bottom of it.

Striving to better, oft we mar what's well.

We that are true lovers, run into strange capers.

Prosperity's the very bond of love.

> . . . so we profess
Ourselves to be the slaves of chance.

Better three hours too soon than a minute too late.

Travelers must be content.

> It is the stars,
The stars above us, govern our conditions.

When Nancy finished reading, Mrs. Roderick remarked, "If that was meant to be a message to me, I can't make head or tail of it."

Ned admitted that he could not fathom the meaning of the conglomeration of quotes. Since Nancy had said nothing, he asked her, "Have you any idea what this means?"

Nancy smiled. "Yes. I think I know."

CHAPTER XIX

A Trap

MRS. RODERICK and Ned waited breathlessly for Nancy's interpretation of the Shakespearean quotations.

As Nancy continued to study the words, Mrs. Roderick said impatiently, "If Miss Drew left that paper for me, how in the world did she expect me to get any message out of it? I'm not familiar with Shakespeare's plays."

"I can't answer that," Nancy replied, "but this is what I think she was trying to tell you. First of all, Miss Drew believes she has fallen in love but she has some doubts."

"I should think she would," Mrs. Roderick said, "if the man she thinks she has fallen in love with is as bad as you picture him."

Ned, interested in Nancy's findings, begged her to go on.

"Well, Miss Drew is about to take a chance anyway," Nancy said.

The others nodded and waited for her to proceed.

"The bride and groom, or the couple, are going traveling, probably by air. I think that was the reference to the stars. And it will be a night flight."

"Why couldn't it be on a ship?" Mrs. Roderick asked.

Ned grinned. "I think I can guess that one. The quotations mentioned that the stars had governed the condition. That could mean weather. If it's a bad night, their plane wouldn't be able to take off."

Mrs. Roderick looked at the list again. "Here's one you haven't told us the meaning of. It says, 'Better three hours too soon than a minute too late.' "

"That is puzzling," Nancy admitted, "but my guess is that Nancy Smith Drew, having some real doubts about the whole thing, wishes that you, Mrs. Roderick, could come to the plane before she flies."

A frightened expression came over the woman's face and she threw her hands into the air. "My goodness, I couldn't go to New York! I'd like to help Miss Drew. She is a lovely person and if she is in trouble she needs help. But I must say she could at least have left me a note I could understand and say good-by and make her request in plain English."

"I have a hunch," said Nancy, "that Edgar Nixon was with her when she came here and the poor girl had no chance to write you an explanation. The next best thing she could do was to put a message in the form of a code and the first thing that came to her mind was Shakespearean quotations."

Mrs. Roderick shook her head. "This is too much for me. Well, I just hope that whatever Miss Drew is going to do she won't be sorry for it. I'm afraid I can't help her, though."

Ned spoke up. "If Edgar Nixon is as slick as you think, Nancy, I bet I know what his next move was. When he got to thinking about the quotations, he'd deduce that you'd come here and find out they had a special meaning. My hunch is that he has already canceled their flight reservations."

Nancy agreed and asked him to telephone the airline and find out. In a few minutes he learned that the reservations for Mr. Nixon and Nancy Smith Drew for the Monday night flight to London had indeed been canceled.

Mrs. Roderick was very upset. "Do you think they are still around here?" she asked.

Nancy shook her head. "By this time Edgar Nixon knows the police are after him. He has probably changed cars again and left Emerson. It's likely he sold his red one to the pal who nearly ran us down.

"He probably went to Ira Nixon's in the new car, stole the thousand dollars, and will meet Miss Drew in New York. Or, if they're already married, she's with him now."

Nancy asked Ned to call other airlines and this time he had good news. He located a new reservation for Nixon and Miss Drew.

"I think," he said, "that Miss Drew couldn't get her passport changed in a hurry, so she's using the one with her maiden name on it."

Nancy sighed. "Even though I may be too late to prevent a wedding, I can alert the New York police where to nab Edgar Nixon."

As Nancy and Ned got ready to leave, tears came to Mrs. Roderick's eyes. "You people are very kind and I do hope you can do something for poor Miss Drew. I'm afraid she has lost her head and has no relative or anybody in this country to help her."

"She has friends," said Nancy, "but I imagine she's too proud to ask their advice."

Ned suggested that they stop at Emerson police headquarters, to see if there was any news of the elusive couple and to ask the chief to notify the New York police.

They were told that there were no leads and the officers were glad that Nancy had one to suggest. Word would be sent to New York immediately.

As Nancy and Ned left police headquarters, she

glanced at her watch. "Oh, I didn't realize how much time has passed. Bess and George and I will be dreadfully late getting home. Ned, would you mind calling Hannah and telling her that I won't be there in time for supper after all?"

"Glad to."

When they reached the fraternity house, George and Bess were waiting with their dates in the hallway. The girls' luggage was piled up.

"We began to think you had gone home without us," George teased.

The couple grinned and Ned said, "Wait until you hear what we've found out." The story was quickly told about the quotations.

Burt burst out laughing. "Say, how about sitting in for me, Nancy, in my Shakespeare class? You might pull an A for me."

It did not take long to load the car. After thanking the boys for a wonderful weekend, the girls jumped in. With a last wave, Nancy drove off.

The journey was uneventful. The girls did not even stop to eat.

"It's so late," said Nancy as they neared the outskirts of River Heights, "how about you girls spending the night with me?"

They agreed, since they did not want Nancy to make the last part of the trip alone. As soon as they reached the Drew home, the cousins phoned their parents.

Both Mr. Drew and Mrs. Gruen had welcomed the girls eagerly. Hannah had prepared some tasty chicken and lettuce sandwiches, a large bowl of fresh cut-up fruit, and a chocolate cake.

As the girls ate, they related the latest items in the mystery. "Amazing!" said Mr. Drew.

Finally Nancy changed the subject. "How's Ira Nixon?"

Her father answered. "I went over there as soon as I got home and heard about the theft. I urged Ira to inform the police, but he still steadfastly refused to do so. He seemed to be calmer, however, so I did not think it was necessary for me to stay or to ask a neighbor to come in."

The three girls began to suppress yawns and Mrs. Gruen suggested that they get to bed as soon as possible. They all slept soundly, but Nancy awoke early with a persisting thought in her mind. She proposed it to Bess and George.

"Girls, if we can get permission, what would you say to going to New York? Nancy Smith Drew will need moral support when the police arrest Edgar Nixon."

George's face broke into a broad grin. "I can't think of anything I'd like better than to see the police nab that cruel man."

Bess said, "If you tell Nancy Smith Drew about her inheritance, maybe she won't feel so bad about having a husband in jail."

The girls came downstairs early and asked Mr. Drew what he thought of the idea.

"It's a good one," he said, smiling. "You may as well see this mystery to its conclusion and you can stay in New York overnight with Nancy's Aunt Eloise."

Nancy, Bess, and George had visited Mr. Drew's sister several times. They adored the school-teacher and she was always delighted to have them visit her.

"She hasn't left for school yet," said Nancy. "Suppose I call her right away."

Nancy had a long talk with her aunt, who was amazed to hear about the case and pleased that the girls were coming.

"I'd love to see you," she said.

As soon as Nancy had eaten breakfast, she phoned the River Heights airport and made a reservation for the three girls on a flight to New York that afternoon. Bess and George went home to get their clothes and Nancy picked them up later. She planned to leave her car at the airport parking lot.

After the girls had purchased their tickets and obtained seat reservations, they sat down to chat. Nancy said, "I'd like to find out how Ira Nixon is and tell him where we're going."

She went off to a phone booth. To her delight she found that Ira Nixon was feeling better and decided not to disturb him with any worry about his brother.

As she left the booth, a young woman walked up to her. "You're Nancy Drew, aren't you? I've seen your picture in the paper lots of times."

Nancy acknowledged that she was.

"I've just come from the powder room," said the young woman. "A friend of yours is in there. She saw you come into the airport. She is terribly ill and asked me if I'd go and find you and bring you back there."

Nancy looked at her watch. Only twenty minutes to plane time!

"All right," she said.

The two hurried to the powder room. Nancy could see no one inside.

"Over here," her companion said, and led Nancy around a corner.

The next instant the strange woman opened her purse and whipped a handkerchief from a plastic bag. She grabbed Nancy around the neck and held the handkerchief tight over the girl's nose and mouth. It had a peculiar sickish odor.

Nancy struggled to free herself, but within seconds she blacked out.

CHAPTER XX

Shattered Bells

"I WONDER what could be keeping Nancy?" said Bess nervously when her friend did not reappear. "Our plane leaves in ten minutes."

"We'd better hunt for her," George suggested. "Maybe she's waiting for us at the gate."

Nancy was not at the gate, nor was she in any of the telephone booths.

"She has the tickets, so I'm sure she wouldn't go without us," Bess remarked. "Let's look in the powder room."

The cousins hurried to it. At first they did not see Nancy, but when Bess peered into the nursery, she gasped. Her friend was lying under a crib, covered with a blanket!

"What's the matter with her? Bess asked, frightened.

"I think she's been drugged," George said grimly.

The girls uncovered Nancy and shook her. She did not respond. Quickly they rolled the crib aside and put Nancy on a couch. Bess rushed to get a towel, held it under the cold water, and put it on Nancy's forehead. George chafed her wrists and gently slapped her cheeks. Finally Nancy opened her eyes.

"What happened to you?" Bess asked.

Nancy blinked and took several deep breaths, but did not answer.

"Maybe we'd better call a doctor and forget the trip," said Bess.

Her statement seemed to rouse Nancy to consciousness. "No, no," she said weakly. "Help me up and I'll be all right."

The girls did not question her further. They knew, without being told, that once more Edgar Nixon had tried to intervene in Nancy's plans and keep her from following him. They were more convinced of this than ever when they found her handbag intact.

Supporting Nancy, the two girls managed to walk her to the plane and onto it. By the time she reached her seat, the dazed girl declared she felt better, and whispered to her friends what had happened.

"We guessed as much," George replied. "Now just take it easy until we reach New York."

Nancy dozed during most of the trip, but by

the time they set down at the airport, she declared she was all right.

"This is really proving to be a dangerous mission," the young sleuth said. "Are you both sure you want to carry on?"

"Of course we do," said George. "But I have a suggestion for you."

George felt that it might be wise for Nancy to try disguising herself.

Bess suggested, "You have on a reversible coat. You can turn it inside out, and tie a scarf over your hair and wear sunglasses."

"All right. I'll do it," Nancy replied.

As soon as the three girls got into a taxi to transfer them from LaGuardia Airport to Kennedy Airport, Nancy took off her coat, turned it inside out, and put it back on. The paisley pattern scarf which she had been carrying in a pocket was tied around her head, so only her face showed. Just before stepping from the cab in front of the airline building, she put on her sunglasses.

George said, "I never finished telling you my idea. Nancy, pretend you've never met Bess and me. You run ahead and do your sleuthing. We'll follow at a discreet distance."

Nancy said she would go to the ticket counter, while the other girls watched the passport desk for Edgar Nixon and Nancy Smith Drew.

"Okay, and if one of us finds out something, we'll raise our handbag in the air as a signal."

By this time Nancy was feeling her normal self and went at once to the airline counter. "Have Mr. Nixon and Miss Drew checked in yet?" she asked.

The clerk consulted his list. "No."

Nancy took a seat nearby where she could watch the arriving travelers. Several who were making the flight to London came to the counter but none was either Edgar Nixon or Nancy Smith Drew.

She was beginning to feel discouraged, when a couple hurried toward the long bench where she was seated. The man told the young woman to sit down and he hurried off to the counter.

"He certainly looks like Edgar Nixon," Nancy thought excitedly.

As she continued to stare at him, she caught a glimpse of a cuff link. It was red with a black star in the center. Instantly Nancy recalled what Mr. Whittier, the River Heights jeweler, had told her—that the man who had purchased a lovely pin for Nancy Drew had bought red cuff links like these for himself!

"I'm sure he's Edgar Nixon!" Nancy decided, and nonchalantly raised her handbag into the air to alert Bess and George.

She now turned her eyes toward the young

woman. Was she the English heiress? Was she married?

Nancy's heart began to beat faster as the woman started to take off her gloves. She wore no wedding ring!

Taking a chance that she had spotted the person for whom she had been searching, Nancy moved over and sat down beside her.

"Pardon me, but aren't you Miss Nancy Smith Drew?" she asked.

The young woman jumped in surprise. "Yes, I am. Do I know you?" she asked.

"No, but first of all let me tell you that my name is also Nancy Drew. I must talk to you quickly. Did you ever receive a letter from England telling you that you have inherited a small fortune?"

"Why, no!" the amazed young woman exclaimed. "How did you know about this?"

"Because the letter came to me by mistake and I have been trying for weeks to find you."

"Do you have the letter with you?"

Nancy shook her head. "It was stolen. Miss Drew, it's a long story, but before I tell you everything, I must know this. Is the man with you Edgar Nixon?"

"Yes."

"You're not married to him?"

"No, not yet. He wanted to marry me right

away and take me to England for a honeymoon, but I told him we would have to wait until we get to London. Even though I have no near relatives, I thought it would seem more like home to marry there."

Nancy took hold of one of Miss Drew's hands and looked straight into her eyes. "I'm dreadfully sorry to have to tell you this. You must not marry Edgar Nixon. He's wanted by the police for robbery and using the mails to defraud victims in a phony Lonely Hearts Club."

The actress gasped "I don't believe it!"

Nancy glanced up toward Bess and George. Both were holding up their handbags and looking toward the counter. Two men had approached Edgar Nixon.

"Look over there, Miss Drew," Nancy said. "Those are plainclothesmen arresting Edgar Nixon."

All the color drained from the actress's face, but she got up when Nancy did and walked with her to the counter.

They were just in time to hear one of the policemen say, "You're under arrest!"

As Edgar Nixon loudly protested, Nancy stepped forward.

"I'm Nancy Drew from River Heights," she introduced herself. Bess and George came up and confirmed the statement. Nancy went on,

"I also accuse this man. He tried to harm me so that I could not frustrate his plans."

The other plainclothesman said that he had arranged for the use of an office in the airport so that they might talk in private. The two policemen marched Edgar Nixon toward it and the others followed. Miss Nancy Smith Drew, trembling, clung to Nancy.

"I know this is dreadful for you," the young detective told her, "but as soon as the shock is over, you will be grateful that you were saved from a very unhappy marriage."

During the conference that followed, all of Edgar Nixon's unsavory schemes were brought out. He admitted having had two men to help him and a girl who had become a friend through his Lonely Hearts Club.

"Why did you steal the letters from your brother's mailbag?" Nancy asked him.

A sneer came over the prisoner's face. He gave a little laugh as he answered. "Tell your father his Mrs. Quigley is a gabby client. She joined my Lonely Hearts Club. The old gal sent me letters five pages long and told me all her business. So I knew exactly when the money was being mailed to Mr. Drew, and—well, I figured I needed it more than she did.

"I was hiding and waiting for a chance to take the letter from Ira, when you stopped in your car and told him you'd give him cocoa at your house. That was my chance."

Edgar said that getting the Nancy Smith Drew letter was pure accident, but he had instantly planned to benefit by it. One of his club members had sent him an Emerson newspaper. In it was an item that the actress was coaching a play at the college. When he read Mr. Bates-Jones's letter, Edgar had hurried to Emerson to make her acquaintance and a couple of days later asked her to marry him.

All this time, Nixon had not looked at his fiancée who was on the verge of tears. He made no apologies to her, and when questioned by Nancy, he said he had intended to keep the knowledge of her inheritance from Miss Drew until after they were married.

"Do you have the thousand dollars with you that you took from your brother?" Nancy asked the prisoner suddenly.

Taken off guard, Edgar Nixon whipped out his wallet and threw it at the girl. "Take this to the old miser," he shouted hysterically. "He never did treat me like a brother."

Nancy looked in the wallet. Besides the money, there were two plane tickets to London.

As Edgar was led away, Nancy Smith Drew burst into tears. "What a fool I've been!" she sobbed. "First I walked out on those fine boys in the Drama Club because of Edgar. But I did peek in at their show before taking the things in my locker. And I never said good-by properly to Mrs. Roderick.

"Edgar kept urging me to hurry with my packing and wouldn't let me write a thank-you note. But while he was carrying my bags down, I managed to scribble a few verses that had a message in them. Edgar didn't know what they meant."

"Nancy figured them out," Bess said proudly.

Miss Drew turned her tear-stained face toward Nancy. "You've been so wonderful. But," she added sadly, "there'll be no wedding bells for me and I had counted on my marriage so much. Oh dear, I don't know what to do!"

As Nancy thought of an appropriate answer, she suddenly realized that this mystery which she had enjoyed so much was coming to a close. The young detective always felt a vacuum in her life when this happened. But the feeling was not to last long. In a short time she would be working on another case, *Sign of the Twisted Candles.*

Nancy put an arm around the actress. "I'll tell you what you should do, Miss Drew," she said, smiling. "Take one of these plane tickets and go to England tonight!"

"Oh, do you think I should?"

Bess and George backed Nancy up in urging the actress to go. "You can have a wonderful time," Bess said, "and forget all your troubles."

Finally Nancy Smith Drew said, "You dear
girls, I can never thank you enough." Then she
began to quote from Shakespeare:

> " 'But love is blind, and lovers
>   cannot see
> The pretty follies that themselves
>   commit.' "

Match Wits with Super Sleuth Nancy Drew!

Collect the Complete
Nancy Drew Mystery Stories®
by Carolyn Keene

Nancy Drew Back-to-Back

Celebrate over 70 years with the World's Best Detective!

Match Wits with The Hardy Boys®!

Collect the Complete
Hardy Boys Mystery Stories®
by Franklin W. Dixon

The Hardy Boys Back-to-Back

Celebrate over 70 Years with the World's Greatest Super Sleuths!